S0-BJI-975

To Sarah, Shawn,
& Scott —
Best wishes!

Paul Montgomery

VALLEY GIRL

by Paula Montgomery
illustrated by Terry Harper

Pacific Press Publishing Association
Boise, Idaho
Oshawa, Ontario, Canada

Edited by Randy Maxwell
Cover by Terry Harper, David Marvin

Copyright © 1989 by
Pacific Press Publishing Association
Printed in United States of America
All Rights Reserved

**Library of Congress Catalog Card Number:
89-60343**

ISBN 0-8163-0849-7

89 90 91 92 93 ● 5 4 3 2 1

To
my parents,
Sam and Carmelita Bailey
for helping instill in me
a writer's virtues:
faith,
hope,
empathy,
and just plain
stubbornness.

ACKNOWLEDGEMENTS

* Hood River County Library for allowing me to camp in their building for countless hours, researching from old copies of *THE HOOD RIVER NEWS.*

* Pete and Betty Berry and David Marvin for their invaluable help and advice.

* Jan Schleifer for her editing expertise.

* "Hazel" for her willingness to share her story with others.

CONTENTS

I

THE SECRET

Mud sloshed around the boots of three girls as they tramped through an orchard. Surrounding them, half-bare trees, knobby and gnarled, stood firm against a breeze that hinted of winter. The year of 1921 was nearly over.

"I can't wait to see Grandma Smith again!" Hazel Weston sang.

"I know!" laughed her friend, Holly Pennington. "You've told me at least ten times at school today. Your grandmother must be a very special lady."

"She is," Hazel said. "My grandmother's a true pioneer woman, one of the first white settlers in the Imnaha Canyon with Indians and rattlesnakes and bears and . . ."

"Hazel," Holly cut in, "do you think Margie and I could meet her? I imagine she can tell great stories about those days."

"Sure!" Hazel replied as she plucked a stubborn leaf from an apple tree.

"The boys are gaining on us," Margie whispered. "We'd better scoot along home."

Hazel caught a glimpse of Harv Hodson and Nicky Cotton taking turns kicking a can up the path.

The girls quickened their pace until they reached Margie's drive. Hazel could see beyond endless rows of fruit trees to the Phillips's house, dwarfed by an enormous barn.

"Bye, Margie! See you at school tomorrow!" Hazel and Holly called together.

They continued their trek up Alameda Road toward Belmont, while the boys took a shortcut and disappeared behind them.

Holly asked, "What time will your grandmother arrive, Hazel?"

"Mom said her train'll reach Hood River about five this evening." Then the girl bounced up and down excitedly. "That's only an hour away!"

Holly looked amused by her friend's antics. "You're really lucky, Hazel."

"What do you mean?"

"Well, you have a grandmother. Both of mine are gone, and now, Mom — she's pretty sick most of the time."

Gray thoughts suddenly swallowed up Hazel's mirth. She knew all about Holly's frail, sick mother, about the many times Mrs. Pennington had hovered near death. Mrs. Weston had confided in Hazel only yesterday that Holly's mother probably wouldn't live much longer.

Hazel puckered her brows, wondering at the guilt she felt. Could it be because she, Hazel Weston, had so much and her friend had so little? Then she remembered —

"I think I know how you feel, Holly. I remember when my Grandpa Weston died."

"You do?"

"Yes, it was quite a shock to all of us. I was pretty small at the time," Hazel explained, "but I'll never forget my wonderful, southern gentleman of a grandpa. Never!"

"That's the way I feel about Grandma Pennington," Holly said. "What about your other grandfather, Hazel?"

"Oh, he died of blood poisoning way back when he and Grandma first settled on the Imnaha," Hazel declared.

"You mean, your grandmother was left alone with her children in that wilderness?"

"Yes!" Hazel answered with pride. "She had a rough time, but she managed to raise her whole family."

"Oh, Hazel, I can't wait to meet her!" Holly exclaimed. "No wonder you're so eager to see her again!"

Hazel grinned at her friend, then waved as she and Holly parted, the Pennington girl turning left toward her house and Hazel skipping to the right on Belmont Drive.

Wisps of brown, shoulder-length hair stuck out of Hazel's stocking cap, tickling her nose with each gust of wind. Her eyes swept the full cricle of Hood River Valley, the "dream valley" her family had found the spring before.

Snow-covered Mt. Hood looked down on her from the south, while majestic Mt. Adams loomed in the northern horizon, across the Columbia River.

Mt. Adams had changed shape since the girl's arrival. On June twenty-third it had been the scene of a gigantic avalanche. A thundering mass of snow and ice gave way, crashing into the Big Muddy Basin below. Hazel hadn't actually seen the avalanche happen, but she saw the space it left behind and read an account in *THE HOOD RIVER NEWS.*

The girl's home came into view, a white one-story house. She smiled, recalling the first time she had explored the place, discovering her very own bedroom. A cream-colored chest of drawers matched the dressing table across the room, while a small, brass bed completed the set. Two over-sized windows faced southwest and let plenty of sunshine into her corner of the house. The perfect room for a nine-year-old girl!

Hazel found the front door enchanting also. Its window was no ordinary pane, but a picture — a covey of quail in the foreground, hiding from a distant hunter.

The Weston place sat between two orchards, and that summer Hazel had learned firsthand what an abundance of fruit the valley produced. She had helped her mother make strawberry jam, can cherries and peaches, make pear butter and apple-sauce until the stone cellar out back bulged with a year's supply of provisions.

Hazel could see the smoke trails made by the chimneys of her neighbors, the Thompsons first, then Hodsons beyond.

Mr. and Mrs. Thompson had offered the use of their telephone, which Mother said they would use "only in emergencies." The Thompsons were a quiet, stay-at-home couple. The only time they left their driveway was for shopping or when Mr. Thompson took his wife to the Baptist church on Pine Street.

The Hodsons had four children. Harv, who had followed Hazel and her friends partway home, was about Hazel's age. His sister, Edith, was four years older, but didn't act grownup and aloof as some eighth graders did. Edith always seemed willing to listen to Hazel. Lenny Hodson was only three, and the baby, Eugene, had just taken his first step.

Margie Phillips's family numbered even more than the Hodsons. Mr. Phillips, a widower, supported seven children, three older than Margie and three younger. Hazel thought red-haired Joey, the youngest of the brood, a charming little fellow. Oftentimes, she wished she had a brother just like him.

If Hazel were going to measure friendship, though, she would consider Holly her best friend. Holly reminded her of Lory, a schoolmate in the town of Joseph. Holly had lovely, golden hair and blue eyes. And Hazel felt secure in their friendship, confident that her deepest secrets were safe with Holly Pennington.

Actually, the Hodsons, the Phillips, and the Penningtons didn't live very close to Hazel, but because her canyon ranch had been situated several miles from her nearest neighbors, these valley friends seemed only a skip and two hops away.

When Hazel reached the back door, her nose told her that Mother was preparing a feast for Grandma Smith. The house overflowed with mingling aromas of good food.

The girl burst into the kitchen. "I'm home, Mom! When does Grandma's train get here?"

"Soon, Hazel!" Mrs. Weston replied from her place at the stove. "Put on your apron and set the table, please. Grandma will be starved by the time she reaches Hood River, and I'd like her to sit right down to supper when she gets here."

"Yes, Ma'am!" Hazel returned, her heart fluttering with anticipation.

Soon she was spreading hand-crocheted lace across the dining room table. She wanted everything to look special for Grandma Smith.

The girl recalled how her grandmother had scoffed at the idea of a dream valley. In fact, Grandma had called it a "pipe dream."

"Wait till spring! Grandma'll love the view," Hazel breathed as she placed silverware beside the dishes.

After the table was set, Hazel heard her father come through the kitchen doorway. He kissed Mother, then said, "As soon as I change out of these work duds, I'll be ready to haul you gals down to the depot." Although he hadn't ridden horseback for nearly three years, Father still talked like a cowboy.

Hazel's parents were proof of the old saying, "opposites attract." Father stood tall, while his wife was short. She kept her long, dark hair swept up into a roll atop her head. Father, on the other hand, didn't bother with his hair, because he had so little left.

It seemed forever to Hazel before she and her parents climbed into their green Buick and drove downhill toward the main part of Hood River. The train depot rested on the town's lowest level.

Upon their arrival they heard a low whistle from the east, which sent shivers of excitement through the girl.

When the engine huffed and puffed to a halt at the station, Hazel watched wide-eyed for her grandmother. Strangers, one by one, clopped down

the coach's steps. Finally, the girl spotted the familiar face of Grandma Smith.

In that moment Hazel forgot all her ladylike manners, bellowed, "Grandma!" and ran headlong into the smiling woman.

"Well, if it isn't my little *Big Enough!*" Grandmother gathered the girl against her coat.

Hazel welcomed the warm, snug feeling, then spoke with an air of importance, "I'm called *Hazel* now Grandma."

"Ooooh?" The woman chuckled. "Well, you'll always be *Big Enough* to me, but I'll try *Hazel* out for a while."

Then the elderly woman hugged her daughter and shook hands with her son-in-law. "Looks like you've done fine without me thus far, Ida!"

Grandma's smiling face suddenly turned sober. "Does Hazel know yet?" she asked.

"Know what?" came Hazel's quick reply.

Mother flashed the girl a Don't-ask-questions look that left Hazel wondering about the secret. She pursed her lips and trudged slowly after her family to the waiting car.

Father drawled, "Yep! Fall has been pretty mild so far, Mom. You're gonna like it here, I'm sure."

Mr. Weston never would have said that if he had known what Mother Nature had tucked up her sleeve.

II
HOLLY'S WORRY

Friday, November eighteenth, dawned a dreary, drizzly day. Heavy clouds hung like a curtain of gray velvet over the valley, as if setting the scene for trouble.

Hazel stood at her front door, peeking through the window picture where quail hid from a hunter. She was waiting until the last moment to rush out of the house and down the walk to the bus.

The bus was actually a truck, which she would see rounding the corner in front of the Hodson place.

"I hope Harv doesn't get on first," she murmured. If she boarded first, she could sit in the cab over the warm engine. Otherwise, she would be forced to ride in back where loose canvas funneled icy air into her face. No amount of mittens and mufflers could keep her warm. "Brrr!" she shivered at the thought as the bus came into view.

"Bye, Mom!" Hazel called. Running to the edge of the road, she stretched to see if the cab was empty. Her shoulders slumped in disappointment when she spotted a bright red cap bobbing in the window. Hazel moaned and climbed into the rear of the cold truck, taking a seat on one of the benches. She sunk deep into her coat as a turtle would into its shell and faced the frigid wind.

Hazel then took heart, knowing her friend, Holly, would board next. Holly would be a ray of sunshine on such a dreary morning — so she thought.

When the blond girl climbed aboard, she turned sad eyes on her friend.

"Is your mother bad again?" Hazel asked gently.

The girl nodded. "She had the worst spell yet. We were all up half the night. Dad went after Doctor Wiley, because Mamma couldn't breathe." Tears oozed from between Holly's eyelids, and she sobbed, "I love Mamma so much. I don't want her to die!"

Hazel felt helpless. She wished for her grandmother, who had a way with tearful girls. But Grandma Smith wasn't there. So Hazel drew in a deep breath and said, "Don't cry, Holly! She's better since Doc Wiley came, isn't she?"

"Well," the girl sniffed, "she *is* sleeping — finally!"

"There! You see? I'm sure she'll be much better by the time you get home this afternoon."

"I don't know, Hazel. Donna stayed home today to take care of Mamma, and Donna had a test. She wouldn't miss a test unless she knew Mamma was still in danger."

Just then the bus slowed and let on two more students, bringing a halt to the conversation. But Hazel slipped her hand into her friend's and squeezed it to let her know she cared.

As the vehicle rocked back and forth, Hazel became lost in thought. She paid no mind to the cold air anymore or schoolmates tumbling on board. She thought only of Holly's trouble, then of her own family. Mom, Dad, and Grandma had always seemed healthy. What if one of them became terribly ill like Mrs. Pennington? Hazel wondered whether she could be as brave as Holly.

Then an idea struck Hazel. "Let's ask the driver to let us off at Rockford Store, so we can walk to school. It's not that far."

"All right," Holly replied half-heartedly.

Hazel tapped on the window. "Rockford, please!"

The girls hiked down the road toward the Barrett schoolhouse. Nicky Cotton followed them at a slower pace.

Hazel always eagerly greeted her teacher, Mrs. O'Brian, a dark-haired lady with laughing eyes. Her class of fourth graders was the largest class that year, so they filled the overflow room at the top of the building. The overflow room also doubled as library, which pleased Hazel, an avid reader.

Now she could see the school's bell tower reaching skyward between the tall, leafless oaks ahead. The school was handsome, she mused — although the one-room schoolhouse on the Imnaha River still held a special place in her heart.

By the time they reached the steps, Hazel noticed that her friend's spirits seemed brighter.

"Look!" said Holly, pointing. "Here comes Margie! She's early for once."

The three girls clustered together and trotted up the stairs to their room's coat closet, Margie chattering all the way.

She had managed to finish her chores early, so she wasn't her usual late self. "I could have ridden the bus, but I think I'd rather walk than have to suffer in that wind machine!"

The girls laughed — even Holly. And Hazel felt pleased that her friend appeared happier.

"I'm looking forward to Thanksgiving," Margie continued.

Thanksgiving! With the excitement of Grandma Smith's arrival, Hazel had forgotten all about the upcoming holiday. "That's right! Next Thursday *is* Thanksgiving!" Hazel said. "We'll have a two-day vacation from school then, won't we?"

Margie hung her coat on a hook. "Yes, and this will be our first year without Mom. But our housekeeper, Mrs. Riley, has promised us a dinner fit for President Harding himself."

Hazel glanced over at Holly. The girl looked sad again. Perhaps she was thinking about her own mother and the possibility of this Thanksgiving being their last together.

Mrs. O'Brian rapped on her desk, bringing the class to order. The girls scurried to their seats, and Hazel made certain that no more was said that day about Thanksgiving or mothers.

A steady drizzle soaked the girls on their way home from school. Because they spent their time dodging raindrops and puddles, they talked little.

15

After Margie turned up her lane, Hazel announced, "Holly, my mother said you could come and spend the night with me sometime."

"Could I, really?" Holly asked.

"Sure! Of course, your folks would have to agree with it."

"Oh, Hazel! Then I could hear one of your grandmother's good stories."

On that note Hazel left her friend, but wondered what Holly would find at home. Would her mother be better, or would Doc Wiley be there again?

A picture of the elderly doctor flashed to mind. A huge man, once so strong, but now a cripple. Hazel knew the story of how his car had bogged down in mud. In his haste to get to an ailing patient, he had lifted the car and injured his back. Ever since, the doctor was forced to use a cane. Hazel thought Doc Wiley a saintly man, willing to leave his warm bed at all hours, always ready with a word of encouragement. Still, he never hid the truth from his patients, and the valley people respected him for that.

Grandma's gasp startled the girl out of her daydream. "Young Lady, you're drenched to the bone! Get in here and into some dry clothes at once!"

"Yes, Ma'am!" Hazel replied, but her mind still lingered on her friend's worry. "Grandma, Holly's mother had a really bad spell last night. The doctor was called, and no one slept."

The woman's voice softened. "I'm sorry, Hazel. Such a young girl to be carrying such a big burden already! But it won't always be that way . . ."

"What do you mean, Grandma?"

"Read the Bible, Girl! Someday all this sickness will be a thing of the past."

Hazel wanted to ask more questions, but Grandma insisted that her wet clothes would cause her an instant case of pneumonia, so Hazel changed into dry things and soon forgot her questions. In no time she was peeling potatoes for supper while her grandmother worked at the cookstove.

A fly buzzed around Hazel's head. She swatted at it with wet hands, but it returned. "Dumb fly! Doesn't he know it's fall — nearly winter? He's not supposed to be here."

Grandma chuckled. "Did I ever tell you about your Aunt Maggie and the flies?"

"No, Grandma!" Hazel picked up the knife again, waiting impatiently for the story.

The old woman began, "Outside the town of Joseph, in the fall of the year, flies gather on the sunny side of the house. They're so thick the wall is just black with them every morning."

"Ew!" Hazel shuddered at the thought of so many flies, but she remembered them well. Dad had told her that the hogs Uncle Emery and Aunt Maggie raised attracted flies. "It's just natural," Dad had declared. "Where there are hogs, there are flies."

Grandma continued, "Maggie had screens on the doors and windows, but the hired help were always coming in and out. Consequently, the flies joined them. Maggie had a terrible time keeping those pests out of her house — the flies, I mean!"

Hazel giggled. She knew what a fussy house-keeper her aunt was. How those flies must have angered her!

"Anyway," Grandma went on, "one morning Maggie got a brainstorm when she gazed out the door at all those flies clinging to her house for warmth. 'Yep!' she said. 'I'll just sweep the whole lot of them into my dustpan and throw them into the stove. That'll get rid of those pesky creatures for good.' So outside she went while the flies were still stiff with cold, and did just that. It took several times to fill her dustpan, but she threw them all into the stove, chuckling like a witch at her shrewdness."

Hazel wrinkled up her nose. She found herself almost feeling sorry for the flies — but not for long.

"Poor Maggie!" Grandma exclaimed. "She had forgotten about the fire going out, and the stove wasn't quite hot enough to kill them. In fact, the warmth brought the creatures to life!"

"Oh, no!" Hazel wailed.

"Yes!" chortled Grandma. "Flies began to march out of that stove by the hundreds, buzzing through her spotless house. Maggie went wild, chasing flies, swatting flies, shooing flies outside. She was miserable."

Although Hazel sympathized with her aunt, the girl laughed until her stomach hurt.

That evening a heavy rain swept through the valley. As Hazel lay awake in her little brass bed, she could hear the wind howling around the house. Many thoughts crowded into her mind — the pitiful look on Holly's face, Margie Phillips with no mother at all, the secret her parents and grand-mother shared.

Outside, the rain turned to sleet, and Hazel could hear it pelting against her window. Finally, she drifted off, and as she slept, the sleet changed to snow, a fast, heavy snow that threatened to engulf the sleeping valley.

III
HOUSEBOUND

A strange cold jolted Hazel awake. As she blinked the sleepiness from her eyes, curious feelings swept through her. "Something's different," she told herself while reaching for her slippers and robe.

She shuffled over to the window, never expecting the sight beyond her curtains. Several inches of snow covered everything, and more was falling, as if a giant pillow had burst over the valley, sending its fleecy contents in every direciton.

Hazel could hear her father loading the stove. "Now, Mom," he said with a chuckle, "don't give me a bad time! I know it's twenty-two degrees out there and still snowing. But, honestly, this is unusual weather for these parts. I'm sure the storm will let up soon."

"Just the same, Tom," came Grandma's voice, "the way that east wind howled last night, I felt just like I was back in the Wallowa Valley."

At breakfast Father ate hastily, then headed outside to shovel a path to the barn where the wood was stored, "just in case."

Hazel sat dabbling at a bowl of hot cereal while she listened to Mother and Grandma talk.

"Even if it snowed another two feet, it wouldn't bother me one bit," the older woman declared. "We've weathered worse than this many a time on the Imnaha. As long as we have wood for the stove and provisions in the cellar, we'll survive." Then Grandma tilted her head questioningly. "Ida, you do have a good supply of kerosene for the lamps, don't you, in case the electricity goes off?"

"Yes, Mom! I also keep plenty of candles on hand. Never have trusted those wires anyway!" Mother laughed. "I'm just like you. No matter how close to civilization we live now, I'll always prepare for winter. Force of habit, I guess!"

Hazel was a jumble of emotions. The subject of her Imnaha days always raised pleasant memories. But what had happened to her dream valley? Were the stories about mild winters false? She welcomed a little snow for sledding, but this storm seemed different to Hazel.

"Silly me!" the girl silently scolded herself, then began clearing bowls from the table.

All day Hazel's father struggled against the storm, keeping the path to the barn clear. Every time he came puffing back inside, his face smarted from the cold, and his eyebrows were frozen white. "Whew! I can hardly keep ahead of it!" he would complain.

Mother and Grandma would hover around him like fussing hens until he warmed enough to return to his task.

And all day Hazel wandered from window to window, watching the falling flakes. Sometimes the east wind would really bluster and send wisps of snow scudding against the house where it formed drifts.

Luckily, Hazel had brought a couple of books home from school, which helped fill the empty hours, but her thoughts strayed often to the storm.

Late in the afternoon the girl took a break from her reading and strolled quietly into the dining room.

Her mother's voice filtered through the kitchen door, "Well, I just don't want Hazel to know yet. There's no use in making her anxious about it so soon."

"Whatever you want, Ida," came Grandma's voice. "But I think you should tell her before . . ." Just then a pan banged loudly to prevent Hazel from hearing the rest.

"What *is* their secret?" Hazel wondered. Now she was truly puzzled. From then on she couldn't concentrate on the book and finally gave up reading.

Father soon stamped snow from his boots for the last time that day. "It should stop any time now," he said.

The storm didn't stop. And when the girl pulled the quilts over her that night, nearly two feet of snow lay outside her window.

The next morning, Sunday, she forgot about her slippers and rushed to look outside. "Ooooh!" she cried. The white mound had risen to the windowsill.

"Daddy!" she called, racing into the living room and almost upsetting his steaming drink. "Daddy, the snow looks like it's over my head!"

"Sure does, Girl! Don't you dare step outside, or it'll swallow you up and we wouldn't find you till spring!" Father ruffled her hair, then told his family, "Mr. Thompson yelled across that the telephone and telegraph wires are down, so there's no contact with the outside world."

Hazel's heart skipped a beat. The entire valley was marooned in a sea of deep, deep snow.

Grandma started to say something, then decided against it. Hazel guessed that she was about to compare this "mild" winter with those in the Wallowa Valley or the Imnaha Canyon.

Snow fell continuously all day, but oddly, it stayed the same depth.

"That's because it's settling," Father explained. "It's getting heavier by the minute. I'm going to have to shovel the roof soon if this stuff keeps up."

"Please, no, Tom!" Mother protested. "Don't go up on that roof! If you should get hurt, we could never get you to the hospital. Not even horses can get around right now."

"Well, I'll wait awhile, Ida, but you'd better hope it doesn't change to rain. If it does, the snow'll soak up the water like a sponge and really get heavy."

"Don't be such a worrywart, Tom!" Mother retorted. "This house is practically new. Surely, they built the roof to hold."

25

Dad sighed. "I hope so, Ida. This house is all we have. With jobs so scarce this time of year, I don't know what we'd use for money to mend it.

Hazel squirmed in her chair and looked up at the ceiling. Later, she peeked out her window at the barn, deciding the barn would surely go first and warn Father before their house caved in. As long as the barn stood firm, she refused to worry.

That night, just minutes after the girl climbed between her icy sheets, drowsiness crept over her. Outside, snowflakes were still falling. They seemed to cover her like an endless, white quilt as she floated off in dreamland.

The next morning Hazel realized it was Monday. "How will I ever get to school? Could you carry me, Daddy?"

Her father burst into laughter. " Hazel, the snow is up to my waist and you want me to carry you all the way to a schoolhouse that isn't even open?"

"It isn't?"

"Of course not!" Grandma chimed in. "How do you suppose the teacher would get there — fly?"

Hazel hadn't thought of that. Teachers are teachers, she figured, and they are always supposed to be at school.

"Did you look outside, Hazel?" Grandma asked.

"Yes! It's still snowing," the girl grumbled.

"Not exactly! You'd better take another look."

Hazel rushed to the window and stared at white pellets that looked smaller than snowflakes. "What is it, Grandma?"

"It's what we used to call 'tapioca snow,' tiny frozen droplets that are turning this valley into one huge sheet of ice."

Hazel's eyes grew large with wonder. As the frozen granules piled up, they did indeed look like tapioca pudding — a very *large* bowl of pudding, that is.

The ice fell continuously all day. Every time father wanted to climb onto the roof, Mother discouraged him. "It's too icy, Tom. Please don't make me upset." And each time, he complied with her wishes.

Father's reaction puzzled Hazel. Ordinarily, he could be quite stubborn. "Maybe he's tired from shoveling the path to the barn and doesn't really want to tackle the roof job," she concluded.

The next morning a deathlike silence fell over the valley just before daybreak. Then a gentle pattering sound swept from the west as the temperature rose. When the rain hit the valley's frozen floor, it turned instantly to ice, forming a treacherous, thicker crust that neither man nor beast dared to walk upon.

Hazel woke to a loud cracking sound, then her mother's shrill cry, "Tom! The roof's caving in!"

"I knew it!" his gruff voice responded. In seconds, the entire family was up and gathered in the dining room. Overhead, an ugly crack split their once smooth ceiling.

The sound came again, and Grandma grabbed Mother. "Ida, you get under this doorway and stay there! Here, I'll get you a chair."

"Oh, Mom! Don't be silly!" Mother reddened.

"If I'm going to save the house, I'll need help," Father said. "Someone will have to go after Charles Phillips while I climb a ladder and see how I can get that ton of ice off our roof before the whole thing gives way."

"I guess I'll have to go then," Mother offered.

"Ida, don't even think of such a thing!" Grandma scolded her. "I'll go."

Mother whirled around. "You? Mom, that is nothing but ice on top of three feet of snow. If you fell, you'd break a leg, and remember, there's no way to get you to the hospital. . ."

Suddenly, Hazel felt three pairs of eyes staring at her.

"Hazel, remember the time you helped Daddy and Uncle Frank save the hay when the big stack caved in.?"

"Yes," the girl replied in a weak voice.

Father looked at her intently and asked, "Do you think you could make it over to Mr. Phillips's house and get his help? He's young and strong and will surely know how to save our roof."

Hazel's tongue felt glued to her teeth. The snow was over her head. What if she broke through the ice? Dad had said they wouldn't find her until spring.

Her father seemed to read her mind. "Don't worry about sinking! After all that ice yesterday and this freezing rain today, the crust is so hard. Anyway, you're light enough not to break through. Your only concern will be to stay on your feet. You can't imagine how slick it is out there."

"Y-yes, Sir!" Hazel stammered.

In minutes Dad had disappeared outside and Mother was fastening Hazel's coat. "Now remember, no dawdling! You won't be able to tell where the road is, so just cut through the orchards, cross Alameda, and head straight for the Phillips place. The quicker the better! Tell him our roof's caving in. He'll know what to do."

"Yes, Ma'am!" the girl squeaked from behind her muffler. The responsibility pressed down like heavy weights on her small shoulders. Everyone was depending on her to bring back Mr. Phillips — in time.

IV
THE RESCUE

Stepping out the back doorway, Hazel came face to face with a white wall of hard snow towering above her head. She felt paralyzed as anxiety and cold gripped her.

"No dawdling!" her mother had ordered. But how could she go anywhere, except to the woodpile in the barn?

Then the girl spotted some steps her father must have chiseled into the ice. Trembling all over, she climbed carefully, righted herself atop the drift, then pointed her toes west, the direction of the Phillips ranch.

Bang crunch! came some sounds from the other side of her house. Hazel turned to see her father on top of a ladder. He was hitting at the roof with something.

"Must be an ax," she guessed, continuing on her way.

Reaching the orchard's edge, the girl blinked in astonishment. She, short-legged Hazel Weston, was walking among treetops! The trees seemed unreal, with their ice-covered branches that looked like jeweled spider webs.

Feeling more sure of herself, she picked up speed through the frozen jungle orchard and was soon to the clear stretch where Alameda Road was supposed to be.

No fences slowed the girl's pace. She simply walked over the tops of them all. If her house's danger hadn't been tugging at her, Hazel would have enjoyed herself. She could have pretended to be a giant on an early-morning stroll, striding over everything in his path.

But this was not the time for pretending. Mother and Grandma were inside a house that might cave in any minute.

Rain still fell, running down her and freezing underfoot. Hazel could see the Phillips's large front door, neatly cleared of snow. Even their roof

terry harper 83

had been shoveled at some time, because only about a foot of snow lay atop it.

When the girl looked up into the clean-shaven face of Mr. Phillips, tears welled up in her eyes, and she spurted out the words, "Our roof's caving in! Daddy needs you!"

"Say no more, Child! I'll be right along."

In no time Mr. Phillips was well-clothed and toting a pitchfork to steady himself on the ice. He started out, quickly passing Hazel.

The girl's anxiety began to fall away as she trotted after the man, trying to keep up with his long strides. In fact, she felt proud that she had reached his home safely, and proud that she hadn't fallen even once until — *whop!* Down she went, landing hard on her pride.

Hazel was too embarrassed to look at Mr. Phillips directly, although he sounded full of concern.

"I'm sorry, Girl. Here! Catch hold of my pitchfork handle!" he offered. So Hazel gripped the tool until she could reach his mittened hand.

In a short while, the man lifted her safely down to her back door. She could hear pounding and crunching sounds overhead.

"Now, Hazel," Mr. Phillips ordered. "You scoot inside that house and stay there. Don't come out for any reason, because when we get this ice chopped in half at the ridgepole, it'll smash everything under it. Do you understand?"

"Yes, Sir!" Hazel gulped, scurrying inside.

Her cold face and toes welcomed the house's warmth as she pulled off her boots.

Grandma came at once. "You made it, Hazel! You've done a brave deed, and I'm proud of you."

"Oh, it wasn't bad," Hazel answered matter-of-factly. I only fell once."

Soon she sat in a doorway across from Mom and Grandma. The older woman had fixed her a hot cup of herb tea, and she sipped it carefully.

Peering into the dining room, Hazel tilted her head to examine the ceiling. It looked ugly, she thought. Their beautiful house was marred. Now, if Mr. Phillips could help Dad save the roof . . .

Bong! the clock boomed, striking nine-thirty and nearly startling Hazel off her chair. Then a cracking sound ripped another crooked line across the ceiling. Hazel glanced at her mother's tightly drawn face. Grandma, however, hadn't flinched. She calmly kept her nose in her Bible and read.

"Nothing would scare Grandma," Hazel thought. "Pioneer women don't scare easily."

Chopping noises on the roof and the monotonous ticking of the clock lulled the tired girl into a light sleep. She dozed until she heard what sounded like thunder. Stiffening with fear, she forced open her eyes. A huge block of ice was crashing to the ground outside the dining room window.

Then a rumble brought the ice down on the west side of the house. Another mountain of ice landed in the yard and lay there like a large, wounded, white animal.

"Whew!" Mother sighed. "Looks like our prayers have been answered another time, Mom!"

"Yes, Ida! Now let's get some food fixed for those poor men. Why, do you realize none of us has had breakfast yet?"

Hazel giggled. She had been so concerned about the roof, she had forgotten completely about her empty stomach. And that was quite unusual for her. "Well," she concluded to herself, "the last four days have been unusual too."

Father was so weary that he went to bed early, and the rest of the family followed his example. The rain had continued all day, but now their roof was safe. Only the ugly cracks splitting the ceiling would remain, a reminder of what could have been.

The next morning, Wednesday, everyone slept in — even Grandma.

Then just before noon, Hazel heard a commotion outside and rushed to investigate. Peering through the window picture, she called, "Daddy! It's Mr. Phillips again. But this time he's trying to drive his team and sleigh."

"You're not joking." Father grabbed his coat and raced outside.

It turned out that Mrs. Pennington was dangerously ill again. Since she needed Doctor Wiley at once, Mr. Phillips had offered to go after the physician. The sleigh, however, had bogged down in the melting ice outside Westons, so he was turning back.

Dad returned to the house, saying, "If the horses started breaking through the ice too, it would cut their legs to pieces. Charles can't chance it."

Hazel's eyes filled with tears. "Then Holly's mother will . . . die," she choked.

"Not if Charles Phillips and I can help it! He's bringing a handsled back with him, and we're going to try to haul Doc Wiley back up on that."

"Tom!" Mother exclaimed. "It's over three miles to the doctor's place. And how will you ever pull that man back up all those steep hills?"

Father stared soberly into his wife's troubled eyes. "Ida, Doc Wiley's a cripple, and the Pennington woman is dying. What if it was you that . . ."

"You're right, Tom," Mother interrupted him. "I'm sorry. I was just thinking how tired you were after yesterday." Then she headed for the kitchen. "I'll fix you a lunch."

Hazel sat next to the front-room window, staring after her father and Mr. Phillips. Both men carried pitchforks and dragged a sled behind them. Their hurried, urgent steps told Hazel that Mrs. Pennington's condition was critical.

How the girl wished to be with Holly now to try and comfort her! But what could she say? She didn't know any Bible texts as Grandma did.

Just then a dripping icicle fell from the eaves and shattered beneath the windowsill. Life seemed as fragile as that icicle to Hazel. Would Holly's mother still be alive when — *if* Doctor Wiley reached the sick woman?

Hazel's worry-filled afternoon passed slowly. The clock struck one . . . then two . . . then three.

The girl recalled how beautiful and welcoming the valley had looked the spring before. But now all that beauty had turned grim-faced and threatening.

Grandma's voice took Hazel away from her dark thoughts. "Fretting about Holly's mother isn't helping her — or you!"

"Oh, Grandma! This valley isn't a dream anymore. It's a — a nightmare! Isn't there anyplace on the whole earth that's trouble free?" Hazel nearly shouted the words.

"Actually, no, Child!" Grandma answered softly. "And there'll never be a place like that — on this old earth, that is. Ever since Adam and Eve ate the forbidden fruit, there could be no more Garden of Edens."

Grandma sat down next to the girl. "Hazel, there's still a lot of good in our lives, all around us if we look for it. We just have to learn to accept the bad with the good." Then the woman smiled. "Someday you'll look back at this afternoon, and it won't seem a smidgen as bad as it does right now."

Hazel turned her doubtful eyes back to the window, then exclaimed, "Grandma! I think I see them. Yes! It's Dad and Mr. Phillips. Look! The doctor *is* riding on the sled!"

"You're right, Hazel!" Then Grandma laughed aloud. "Ida, come and see! That has got to be the funniest sight — two men pulling that huge doctor on a child's sled!"

Mother came at once, but she didn't laugh. She looked greatly relieved that the men were safe.

Mr. Weston waved as he passed the house. The sky was darkening behind him. Would the doctor be in time to save Mrs. Pennington? Hazel would have to wait another two hours to find out.

At last, after the girl had dressed in her nightgown, Father came through the back door, his

41

face red with cold. His first words were, "Doc says he thinks she'll make it. He's going to stay with Penningtons tonight." Then Mr. Weston caught his own joke and laughed. "Couldn't go anywhere if he wanted to!"

"I'm glad she'll be better soon," Mother said, then cried out, "Tom, you're shivering!"

"I'm not cold, Ida, just shaky from all that exercise. I thought I was a strong man until yesterday and today." He sighed deeply. "This snow is a real contest. I was afraid a time or two it just might beat this old cowboy."

Grandma called from the other room. "I just remembered something — do you know what tomorrow is?"

"Yes," replied Mother, "it's Thursday, November twenty-fourth."

"It's Thanksgiving!" Grandma said. "And we have plenty to be thankful for, that's for sure!"

Mother smiled warmly at the older woman. "You're so right. Mom. Our house is safe, and Mrs. Pennington should make it for another Thanksgiving . . ."

Father interrupted her, "Not everyone is as lucky, Ida. I heard lots of news from Doc Wiley today."

"What kind of news, Daddy?" Hazel asked anxiously.

"I'll tell you all about it tomorrow. I'm beat!" Mr. Weston headed for his bedroom.

In minutes the house was dark and quiet. Only the ticking of the clock could be heard.

Hazel lay awake thinking about her long day. Grandma had said she could find some good in it if she looked. She thought and thought until it came to her — "Dad and Mr. Phillips!" *They* were the good — hiking the long distance to town, then pulling heavy Doctor Wiley up those steep hills. Next she considered the proud, old doctor. Surely, people must have peered out their windows at him and laughed. How humiliating for a professional man like him! But he was willing to suffer the humiliation in order to help save a woman's life.

Hazel's young heart swelled with a new love for her father, even for Mr. Phillips and the doctor. Grandma had been right, as always. Hazel did find the good.

She tugged at her quilt and closed her eyes for sleep, all the while wondering about the news Father would share the next morning.

V

AFTER THE STORM

"Don't eat too much for breakfast!" Mother warned the family. "I want everyone to enjoy our Thanksgiving meal, even though we can't get to the store for some of the fancy things we usually have."

Hazel could hardly keep quiet. She was anxious to hear her father's news.

At last Dad finished his oatmeal. "Ida, do you remember that new house on Tenth and Columbia that we admired so?"

"Yes," Mother replied as she cleared away some of the dishes.

"Well, it looks like a cyclone hit it. The whole house collapsed under the weight of snow."

"Oh, Tom!" Mother turned pale and sank into a chair.

"I know, Ida. My stomach turned inside out when I saw it. I thought to myself, that could have easily happened to our place the other day."

"Well, then," Grandma spoke up, "this is truly a *Thanksgiving* Day, isn't it?"

Hazel shuddered at all the "what if" thoughts that raced through her head.

"Oh, that's not all I saw," her father continued. "Apparently, the skylight of Justice Onthank's office gave way and filled his building with snow. What a mess that was to clean up!"

"What about the telephone and telegraph wires, Tom?" Mother asked. "Are they still down?"

"It may be a while before they can be fixed. There are drifts some thirty feet deep in places. That tapioca snow was the worst culprit. It seems the stuff swept down mountainsides and piled up on the highway and railroad. Of course, wires went down at the same time. It will be at least a week before they can clear the tracks between here and Cascade Locks. Doc Wiley said that over three hundred men were working to clear the way, but their progress was mighty slow."

Father laughed heartily. "That good old doctor! For a man so crippled, he's still the best source of news around. He even knew what was going on across the Columbia River."

"Did White Salmon get as much snow as we did, Daddy?" Hazel wanted to know.

"According to Doc, they got even more. At Husum an apple-packing plant collapsed and so did some other apple houses out there."

"Oh, no!" Mother groaned. "Just think of all that good fruit ruined!"

"Ida, we've had several packing houses go down on this side of the river also. I doubt that we'll know the full extent of the damage until the roads are passable, and all the news can get in."

"What about injuries, Tom?"

"Now that's one bright spot. With all the collapsing roofs and travelers stranded on the highways, there's been some frostbite and exposure, but not much else. Of course, we won't know all the news for a while.

"Doc said that the grocery stores are already running out of certain foods," Father continued. "They've decided not to sell large amounts to anyone until trucks can get through from the outside world again."

Hazel strolled over to the window and stared out at the valley, stretching bleak and still, to the eastern mountains. Not a sign of life appeared anywhere. No people, no horses, no dogs — not even a bird.

Waves of loneliness rolled over the girl until she noticed thin smoke trails rising from neighboring houses. The thought of people inside swept away her gloom.

Hazel wondered about the Hodson children. What were they doing cooped up for so long? And would they have a Thanksgiving feast today also?

Then the girl thought about Margie Phillips and her family. Would Mrs. Riley still prepare that meal fit for the President?

"Like I said before," Grandma broke into her thoughts, "as long as that cellar out back is well stocked and there's plenty of wood in the barn, we don't have to worry about any old grocery stores running out of food."

"I hate to spoil your good mood," Dad said, "but the woodpile has really dwindled since the last cold spell. I sure hope Butch Krause can get through soon with another load for us."

As if to read their minds, the wood man dropped by Westons that very morning. The large, strapping frame of Mr. Krause came ambling into their dining room. He handed his coat and hat to Mom, then settled down by the stove.

"Whew! Some snow, huh, Tom?" Mr. Krause began. And soon news flew back and forth, each man informing the other of what he had learned about the storm.

Hazel's nose twitched at the flavorful smells spilling out of the kitchen each time Mom or Grandma opened the door. The girl knew she should be helping the womenfolk with their task, but curiosity kept her at Mr. Krause's feet, where she listened intently to his every word.

Mother had said the wood man was a lay preacher, but he usually avoided the subject of religion with Father. Mr. Krause did tell good stories, though.

"I was wondering how everybody's fuel supply was, Tom," the man's jolly voice boomed. "So I thought I'd work up an appetite for the wife's big meal by tramping around the countryside."

Father told Mr. Krause about his trip to town for Doctor Wiley.

The big man frowned. "I'll go over there next and check on Mrs. Pennington. I'm glad to hear she's better. A blessing, that lady is! Studies the Word everyday. I don't know how she keeps going with all that pain. . ."

49

Father cleared his throat and changed the conversation. He was concerned about the orchards, if cold temperatures had done much damage.

Mr. Krause said the trees looked good thus far. Then he told about a trapper missing upvalley.

Abruptly, the huge man jumped up and donned his coat. "As soon as I can get my truck down the road, I'll be by with wood for you, Tom. Never know how this winter will turn out!"

Dad chuckled. "Well, I'd rather do without any more storms like this last one. I'd told Mom here that winters are fairly mild in this valley."

Butch Krause turned and grinned at the older woman. "Believe me, Ma'am, this is an unusual winter for these parts. . . Goodbye now!"

Hazel looked after the giant man tramping toward the west. How she wished she could run after him and climb atop his broad shoulders and ride to Holly's house!

When she shared her wish with Grandma, the woman laughed, "Is this my little Big Enough, canyon girl? I don't believe it. Why, you must be getting spoiled with all this socializing. You were raised in a wilderness, Girl, hardly ever seeing other children — except on the Fourth of July — until you started school. Now you can't stay snowed in more than a few days without getting fidgety.

Hazel smiled and suddenly felt better. Grandma was right. She really was getting spoiled. She did enjoy having her friends so close. In fact, she was itching to see Holly and Margie again.

On Monday a chinook began to blow, causing the mounds of snow to shrink.

"If that breeze continues a few days," Father commented, "the roads will pack down good enough for traffic — and school," he added with a gleam in his eye.

"Do you think so?" Hazel asked eagerly.

"Maybe Wednesday," he guessed.

As predicted, the bus pulled up at Hazel's house Wednesday morning. But the bus wasn't a bus, nor a truck. It was a large sled, drawn by four sleek, black horses.

Hazel bounced into the empty sled and grinned all the way to Holly's house.

When the two girls met, they hugged each other, and then began to talk. They talked about Holly's mother, about Doctor Wiley's unusual ride, about roofs caving in, and about every scrap of news they could think of.

More children tumbled aboard, adding to their mirth and chatter. And soon the many young voices swelled to such a din that the valley must have thought spring had come early and a great flock of magpies was jabbering across the countryside.

The following Friday after school, Hazel noticed *THE HOOD RIVER NEWS* lying on a chair. Scanning the front page, she read the headlines:

TRAINS 12 AND 17 IN HEAD-ON SMASH

COLUMBIA HIGHWAY UNDER DRIFTS

LOCAL MEN FIGHT SNOW AND ICE

Then Hazel skipped to a small section below:

SNOW HEAVIEST ON RECORD HERE

... According to experiments carried out, that granulated ice which fell almost without intermission on Sunday and Monday of last week weighed 40 pounds to the cubic foot. Leroy Childs of the meteorological bureau, states that the snowfall was the equivalent of nine inches of rain.

The snow which accumulated during the storm on a set of outside scales downtown, weighed 3,300 pounds.

"Ooooh!" Hazel cried out, her eyes drawn again to the cracks that split the dining room ceiling. A tinge of pride surged through the girl when she remembered how she was the only one who could go after Mr. Phillips.

That weekend proved to be a fun-filled one when neighbor children, equipped with sleds and all manner of sliding devices, scrambled out of their houses. On Sunday, Hodsons joined in the sledding. And even Edith, the oldest, frolicked like a first grader.

Small, red-haired Joey Phillips thought himself quite smart when he discovered Westons's cellar door. It slanted just right for his own personal sliding ramp. Up he climbed, then, "Weeee!" down he slid until — *kaplunk!* He landed hard.

"Tut! Tut!" called Hazel as she passed him with her sled, heading toward the field behind her house.

Because the ice was thawing, the older children were bogging down in places, but lightweight Hazel sailed past them all. "Ha! Ha!" she called until — *bang!* She crashed right into a tree.

"Tut! Tut! and Ha! Ha!" scolded a small voice from inside her.

Hazel was so wrapped up in play that she hardly noticed the soreness in her throat. But later, while helping with supper, she found swallowing to be difficult. The girl didn't complain, though, for fear of missing school. She was looking forward to snowball contests at recess. Fortunately for Hazel, she was still young enough not to be called a

tomboy. The older girls, however, had to act ladylike and watch wistfully from the schoolhouse.

Later, at supper, sharp-eyed Grandma guessed the problem. "Not eating as much as usual, Hazel! Does your throat hurt?"

"Just a little bit, Grandma."

After an inspection the woman said, "Tom, her tonsils are badly infected again. I think you should take her down to Doc Wiley's. This girl has had tonsil problems much too long. Something should be done about them."

"We'll do that tomorrow — first thing, Mom!" Dad promised.

Hazel's stomach churned. She had met Doctor Wiley several times, but never as a patient. Mom or Grandma had always taken care of her ills. She wondered — what did a doctor do for infected tonsils anyway, and would it hurt?

A long-faced Hazel was ordered to bed, where she worried more about her appointment with the doctor.

Then she began to wonder about Grandma and Mother's frequent whispering. "They're probably discussing the big secret, whatever it is," Hazel grumbled to herself.

Suddenly, she sat bolt upright. "My tonsils! Maybe the secret is about my bad tonsils. . ."

VI
THE OPERATION

Monday morning came too soon for Hazel. She wiggled nervously while Mother braided her hair into two short plaits, all the while advising the girl on proper behavior at a doctor's office.

"Nothing is more embarrassing than to have a half-grown girl bawl and carry on like a heifer at branding time!" the woman declared, then noticed her daughter's offended look. "Of course, you'd never do such a thing."

"Of course not!" Hazel said primly.

Before the girl could protest, her father scuttled her off to the car, and away they drove toward

57

town. The steep, snow-packed streets made driving hazardous, so the two Westons walked down the few remaining hills to the doctor's office.

In no time the physician was examining Hazel's throat while she uttered an unseemly, "Aaagh!"

"I tell my patients to say 'Ah' in order to give them something to do, Miss Weston. It must get pretty boring just standing around with their mouths open."

Hazel giggled and relaxed — but not for long. The doctor's next words were far from funny.

"Tom, since this problem has been giving her trouble for years, it won't get any better. I think you should consider an operation."

An operation! Hazel gulped. She wished she could close her eyes and disappear, tonsils and all. In the next breath, she took heart, knowing that operations were costly, and Dad was between jobs. Maybe they couldn't afford the surgery. Then Hazel could wait until some later time — much later, she hoped.

She suddenly became aware that the doctor was addressing her. "I asked, when is your Christmas vacation?"

"I think it starts on the twenty-second, Sir," she answered weakly.

The physician eyed his calendar. "Well then, let's plan on taking out those tonsils on Friday morning, the twenty-third." He turned back to the girl. "Don't look so worried, Hazel! You'll feel much better when those troublesome things are gone."

"Yes, Sir," came the girl's shaky but polite reply.

That afternoon Lucy Trent dropped by the Westons with some homework for the sick girl. The two schoolmates didn't know each other well, but since Lucy lived nearby, Mrs. O'Brian suggested she deliver the books.

Thanking Lucy, Hazel looked at the top of the stack — *spelling*! "Ugh!" she grunted. Hazel detested that subject. Although she read a lot, she never could remember when the "i" came before the "e," nor all the other pesky little rules, invented for her annoyance.

"Why isn't my geography book here?" she wondered aloud.

Lucy grinned. "Mrs. O'Brian said you didn't need to study your geography. You already know too much."

Hazel blushed. Geography *was* her favorite subject. In fact, she would race through her lessons at school, finishing long before her classmates, in order to read the *NATIONAL GEOGRAPHIC* magazines in the library.

"I'm sorry you're sick, Hazel, and I hope you get better soon," Lucy said, opening the front door to leave.

"Thank you! I'll get better as soon as the doctor takes out my tonsils at Christmastime."

"Won't you be back to school before then?"

"I think so, whenever my throat stops hurting."

A week later the girl returned to school. All went well until Friday, when the temperature outdoors dropped to sixteen degrees.

"I don't think Hazel should go to school today and chance getting tonsillitis again before her operation," Grandma declared. "After all, it's only a week away."

So Hazel was confined again to the house and her room. A cloudy sky kept the sun from shining through her windows, making the white furniture look a drab gray, the same color as the girl's thoughts.

By Saturday night a stiff easterly wind began to blow, and on Sunday morning Hazel awoke to snowflakes. Her heart fluttered with new hope. "Maybe if we get another bad storm, I won't need to have the operation yet!" she thought, then scolded herself for such selfish thinking. She certainly didn't want to repeat the near tragedy of the Thanksgiving-week snowstorm.

All day snow fell until it lay six inches deep.

Monday the thermometer dipped to twelve degrees, the lowest temperature that winter, according to Father.

"If it stays this cold, you'll be having one long vacation, Hazel, until after the first of the year," Mother informed the girl.

Hazel managed a weak smile. What fun would a vacation be if she were cooped up inside?

Tuesday more snow fell, and with each flake, Hazel's hopes mounted. Maybe she wouldn't be able to get to the hospital after all.

But sleighs and cars kept passing in front of the house, packing down the road into town — just to make certain she would have her tonsils out, Hazel thought.

That evening Father exclaimed, "It's mighty cold out there, Ida! Do you know that ice is clogging up the Columbia River, so much so, that boats can't get through this side of Cascade Locks? And The Dalles ferry is out of commission until the air warms up."

"How can such a big river freeze over, Daddy?" Hazel asked.

"Oh, the whole river isn't frozen over yet, Girl. The shore ice is reaching out into the mainstream. Ice floes are dangerous when they buck into a boat. Could sink one in short order!"

Hazel longed to ride down to the river and see the ice for herself. She really wanted to get out of the house awhile, even if the weather was unbearably cold.

Friday morning the dreaded time arrived. Hazel kissed Mother and Grandma goodbye, then followed with lagging steps behind her father. The icy air slapped at her face, but oddly, the girl felt as if she was sleepwalking. Her entire stay in the hospital proved that way — dreamlike.

Hazel looked tiny in the long ward crowded with beds. Nurses, dressed in starched white uniforms, asked questions and took her temperature.

Soon she was riding on a cart up the hall and through two big doors. A different nurse gently placed a mask over Hazel's mouth and nose. Breathing in and out, the girl quickly drifted off to sleep.

Once, through bleary eyes, she spotted her father. She tried to speak to him, but a misty-like form spread over her, pulling her back into dreams.

The next thing she felt was her father's strong arms lifting her, then the biting cold, the car

whirring beneath her limp body, and at last, her father's arms again.

She forced open her eyes when she sensed the warmth of the Weston kitchen.

Grandma beamed down at her. "Just you see, Hazel! You'll start growing now that those tonsils aren't poisoning your system anymore. Mark my words — you'll grow!"

Hazel tried to smile, but her mouth and throat felt full of sand. Sinking back to sleep, she didn't know that Mom and Grandma were tucking her in her little brass bed.

By Christmas morning Hazel was well enough to sample some of Grandma's invention for "tonsil holes." She called it "snow cream." Hazel had little idea of the ingredients, but the snow cream tasted delicious.

"If only it didn't hurt so much to swallow!" she complained to herself.

Mother, who was well aware of her daughter's favorite pastime, brought the girl a Christmas present. "Harv Hodson was selling these, so I ordered one from him," the woman explained.

Hazel fumbled with the tissue wrapping. "Thank you, Mom!" the girl squeaked, hugging a thick book to her heart. *UNCLE BEN'S COBBLESTONES*, the title read.

Soon she was lost in Uncle Ben's world of bees and birds and bugs, happily learning about nature and its Creator.

On the following day, Monday, Belmont Drive came alive with children's voices. The entire Phillips brood coasted by Hazel's window, grinning and waving from their sleds.

Little Joey tried again to slide down Weston's cellar door — just once! The Hodsons also whizzed by, all but Edith, who dropped in for a short visit.

"How's your throat doing, Hazel?"

"I'm lots better, thank you!"

Edith looked deep into the girl's eyes. "Did it hurt terribly?"

"I don't know. I slept most of the time," Hazel replied.

"I'm going to become a nurse some day," Edith stated matter-of-factly. "I've always wanted to become a nurse."

Hazel piped up, "My grandmother's a nurse, sort of, although at times she's been more like a doctor."

"Do you think you'd like to become a nurse too?"

"Yes, Hazel said, "I would!"

"Good!" Edith squeezed the girl's hand. "Then maybe we can practice together someday."

After Hazel nodded her approval, Edith left the younger girl to watch the fun outdoors.

Hazel looked out the window, but her eyes saw another place, another time when she lived on the outskirts of Joseph. She had been sick for days, and just when her spirits dipped to their lowest, Aunt Maggie popped in and told wonderful stories. Now she lived hundreds of miles away from Aunt Maggie, who had no inkling her niece was in the same, sorry predicament.

The roar of a truck engine startled the girl. Butch Krause was delivering the promised load of wood. Hazel raced to her bedroom window and watched Dad and giant Mr. Krause carry wood into the barn.

Later, the men came inside. "Let's go into the dining room and warm ourselves by the stove, Butch," Dad said.

"Don't mind if I do, Tom!" Mr. Krause sat down. "I hope you'll forgive me for waiting so long with your wood. With this cold spell, I've been working round the clock, and there were several others in greater need."

"Don't mention it! We understood," Dad replied.

Grandma brought in steaming cups of herb tea, then sat down next to her daughter, who was knitting. They, like Hazel, enjoyed Butch Krause's company. He always had something interesting to tell.

"I'm surprised there wasn't any looting of fruit when those packing sheds caved in," Mr. Krause exclaimed. "Of course, no one could get around in that deep snow. So, in that respect, it was a blessing, I suppose." The man spread his huge hands before the stove. "I remember when it wasn't safe to travel between here and The Dalles. There was at least one highwayman who terrorized that stretch of road."

"When was that, Butch?" Father asked.

"Oh, it was way back when our only means of transportation was a team and wagon. We'd just sold our property in The Dalles and had to sign final papers there. I didn't know how I would ever get the money from that town to this one safely. To make matters worse, we had to camp overnight beside the road."

Hazel looked puzzled. The Dalles wasn't too far from Hood River. Why would he have to camp?

Mr. Krause answered her unspoken question with, "Back then the trip took pretty long, because the trail wound through the hills, and people camped partway between The Dalles and Hood River. Our ranch is way over here on the west side of the valley, you know. We just couldn't make it back before nightfall."

The visitor took a sip of his hot drink, then continued, "While we were in the city, we came across some Indians selling huckleberries. So my wife decided to buy enough to fill her large preserving barrel to the top. By the time we finished shopping for flour and cornmeal, it was afternoon. I then headed the team west, and I don't mind admitting I was one, scared fellow — carrying so much money on the open road."

"I can imagine!" Grandma declared.

"When I told my wife that, she suggested that I give her the money. 'Don't ask me where I'm hiding it, Butch,' she said, 'just give it to me!' So I did."

Hazel's eyes widened as she listened intently.

"Well, we traveled as far as we could until it got so dark we had to camp up in the hills. And sure enough! As soon as we settled down, along came the dreaded highwayman, demanding our money.

"I gave him the few bucks I had in my wallet, and he laughed. 'No!' he yelled. 'I want the big money, Mister! Now, tell me where it is!' "

Father broke in, "So he knew about the land deal somehow."

"I'm sure of it, Tom," Butch Krause said. "I felt a bit uneasy standing there with my nose three inches from a gun barrel. Believe me, I sent up a multitude of prayers in those few moments. Then I answered him, 'I honestly don't know where the money is.' It wasn't a lie, because I really didn't know. My wife's a wise woman. She knew I wouldn't lie for any reason."

Hazel wanted to ask, "Not even to save your life?" but she didn't.

"Anyway, that robber went crazy. He tore everything in our camp to pieces, looking for that money. Then, all of a sudden, some noise sounded from the road, and he skedaddled fast."

Hazel forgot her manners this time and asked, "What was the noise?"

"Young Lady, to this day, I don't know. There was no one out there. I sometimes wonder if the Lord sent some noisy angels along to save both our money and our hides, because that fellow was so angry he was nearly breathing fire!"

Now Father was the curious one. "Tell us, Butch, did your wife show you where the money was hidden?"

"No! She wanted to wait until we got to the bank in Hood River first. And you'll never guess where it was all the time."

"Where?" the listeners asked.

"At the bottom of the preserving barrel, under all those huckleberries! The money was a bit stained, but still good." Then Mr. Krause roared with laughter. "Yep! The Lord indeed takes care of His own. He took care of me simply by giving me such a wise wife."

Hazel laughed too, not because of the story, but because her father had just listened to a sermon without realizing it.

"Hazel," Mr. Krause added, "I almost forgot to tell you, Holly Pennington sends her love and hopes your throat will be completely well by the time school starts again."

"Thank you, Mr. Krause! Thank you!" Hazel beamed. What a fine day! First, there came a visit from Edith Hodson, then a story from Mr. Krause, and now a message from dear Holly.

After the wood man left, Hazel caught a glimpse of something yellow in her mother's knitting basket.

"Mom, isn't that stocking awfully small for me?"

"It's not a stocking, Hazel. It's a baby bootie."

For little Eugene Hodson?"

"Noooo," Mother singsonged, "for our little one."

Hazel's mouth flew open in surprise, and she stumbled over her words, "Mom, are — are we having a baby? Is — is this the big secret you've kept from me all this time?"

Mother nodded, smiling.

Hazel hopped around the room. "We're having a baby! We're having a baby!"

"Hazel!" Grandma scolded. "You settle down this instant, or you'll wind up in the hospital again!" The woman's voice sounded stern, but there was a twinkle in her eye.

Hazel obeyed, plopping down next to her mother, looking eagerly into her face. "Will it be a boy or a girl?"

"We'll know when the baby comes."

"When will that be?" Hazel wanted to know.

"Not until May."

The girl frowned. "May? Can't we have the baby sooner?"

"I hope not!" Mother laughed. "I have a lot more knitting to do before he or she gets here. It's been a long, long time since we've had a baby around — almost ten years, you know." Suddenly, Mother's voice took on a serious note. "Hazel, I think you'd better lie down for a while. You've had too much excitement for one day."

71

"Yes, Ma'am!" Hazel happily agreed and skipped into her bedroom. "A baby! A real baby! she breathed.

But May seemed so far off.

VII
TRAPPED

Hazel's indoorsy skin tingled at the cold fresh-
ness outside.

"I've missed school soooo much!" the girl
exclaimed to her best friend.

"Even spelling?" Holly teased.

"Almost!" Hazel replied.

With lightning speed, the girls ducked in time to
miss flying ice chunks the horses kicked their way.
The sled-bus had once again filled with noisy,
eager children's voices as it weaved through frozen
orchards and grasslands toward school.

73

VALLEY GIRL

Although Hazel promised to stay in at recess times that first week, she still enjoyed every minute of school. She felt as frisky as a puppy on a spring morning. Of course, spring hadn't arrived, but she knew the worst part of winter was behind her.

The following Sunday, a chinook blew in, pushing the mercury well above forty degrees. By Monday all the icicles lining Hazel's house had disappeared, and the truck-bus returned to take the sled's place.

Snow still surrounded the school's playshed where Hazel ran wild at recess, enjoying games like Fox and Geese and Pom Pom Pullaway.

Soon warm rains began melting the mounds of snow around the valley, and one day near the end of March, Hazel happened to glance at the newspaper which read:

> On Friday afternoon of last week, according to residents who drove over the Columbia Highway by auto, all snow was cleared for the full width of the paving, and for the first time since November 20 of last year, the road was open for autos to pass at all points. . .

Hazel whistled under her breath. "It's taken over four months to completely clear the highway to Portland!" she mused.

As winter's curtain fell away, Hazel noticed the damage left behind — the uprooted trees, over-turned fences, collapsed sheds, all reminders of the worst snowstorm in decades. But with April, the greening valley made the harsh months seem foggy and faraway.

Every morning Hazel delighted in sights along the roadway, such as shy calves peeking at her from behind proud mother cows, and wobbly-legged colts frisking alongside their mothers. Leaves appeared gradually, then buds. By the middle of May, delicate blossoms of apple, pear, and cherry trees covered the countryside with their lacy beauty.

One warm spring afternoon Hazel found her grandmother at the east window.

"Yes, Young Lady," the elderly woman admitted, "this is indeed a *dream* valley!"

Hazel beamed up at her grandmother, then gazed beyond the orchards to the mountains where snow still lingered in draws. "Grandma," Hazel's voice sounded impatient, "when will Mom have the baby? I'm getting tired of waiting."

The woman chuckled. "So is your mother." Then she ruffled the girl's hair. "It won't be long now, Hazel."

Saturday morning, May twentieth, Mrs. Weston stayed in her room instead of coming to breakfast.

Hazel could feel the tension in the air as Grandma said, "Tom, don't stray too far from the house! We'll need you to go after Doc Wiley before long."

Hazel missed her mouth with the spoon. "May I go too?"

Grandma's eyes twinkled. "You are going to the Phillips place today. Arrangements have already been made."

"Aw, Grandma! I want to be here when the baby comes."

The old woman smiled sympathetically. "I'm sorry, Dear, but you'll be better off at the Phillips place."

"Yes, Ma'am," Hazel muttered.

As soon as the meal ended, Hazel was scuttled outside along with the promise that Father would fetch her from Margie's house as soon as the baby arrived.

The girl tripped through the grass, chanting, "We're having a baby!" All the birds seemed to sing with her as she wandered through the leafy orchard where blossoms, white and withering, swirled along her pathway.

The Phillips children, already finished with their morning chores, were waiting for Hazel at the barn.

"Your father dropped by really early," Margie said, "and asked if you might stay with us today." Her face lighted with the question, "What do you want, Hazel, a boy or a girl?"

"That's simple! I want a baby brother just like your little Joey!" Hazel exclaimed.

Although Joey's freckled face turned the same color as his hair, he did look pleased.

Soon the children were playing tag in the barn and around the house. When they tired of that game, they decided to play hide-and-seek.

"Da barn's full of goody hiding places!" Joey announced to the visitor.

Hazel gave the boy an approving smile.

The first few rounds of hide-and-seek, Hazel was caught. Then she found a special, secret place. Inside the barn's big double doors, hay was stacked along the wall. Hazel had discovered a hole just her size down between some bales. From then on, others were caught, but never Hazel. She could spy from inside her secret hiding place, and when the way was clear, jump out and touch the barn door, which was home base.

"Free!" Hazel called with glee.

Buddy Phillips spun around. "How did you do that again, Hazel?" he demanded.

"I'll never tell!" the girl sang out.

Next, when little Joey was "It," Hazel waited until the others were out of sight, then quietly slipped down into her hole.

"Sometimes being small has its good points," she told herself smugly.

Then, without warning, a herd of children stampeded over the top of her hole, three squealing youngsters dashing for home base. Down tumbled a bale of hay, locking Hazel into her secret place.

At first the girl's head whirled from the suddenness of the mishap. Scrunched into a lopsided ball, she could hardly move. She could hear the children all chattering at once, trying to guess her whereabouts.

"Help! I'm in here!" she called. But the Phillips children only chattered more as they moved farther outside.

Then Buddy announced, "Maybe Hazel got tired and went back to the house."

"Or maybe her father came to get her," Margie suggested. "That's not like Hazel, though, to go off without saying goodbye. . ."

"I'm in here! I'm in here!" But no one heard the squeaky little voice from inside the barn.

Was this to be her end? What a place to die! She wished she could transform herself into a cow and eat her way out. That thought made her giggle in spite of her predicament.

A sudden wave of courage shot through her veins. "I may be small, but I'm no quitter!" the girl told herself as she began to claw at the heavy bale overhead. Her fingers worked into the hay. Then she pushed with all her might. Finally, after much effort, a bit of fresh air filtered through to her sweating face.

Hazel's back ached from stiffness, her neck felt twisted, and her fingers stung from the prickly hay, but the fresh air seemed to renew her spirits, and she worked harder.

Inch by inch the heavy bale moved until there was a hole just big enough for the girl to squeeze through. At that moment, she heard the house-keeper's voice calling the children to lunch.

Taking a step, the girl was startled at her own weakness. She made her way slowly to the house.

Margie answered her knock. "Hazel! Where've you been?" Then she noticed the hay sticking out of the girl's tousled hair. "You sure look funny!"

Hazel mumbled, "Well, I don't feel funny. You and your brothers knocked a bale over on me, and I was trapped."

"I'm sorry," Margie said, her amusement turning to concern. "Come and wash up! You can use my comb. Mrs. Riley would never let you up to the table, looking like that!"

Although the housekeeper was somewhat strict, Hazel admired the woman. She had the spunkiness of Grandma Smith. Always busy, she kept the entire Phillips clan well dressed and well fed.

In minutes the large dining room filled with youngsters of all sizes. Even little Joey's freckles had been freshly polished before he climbed into his place.

As they finished eating, there came a knock at the door. A hush fell over the flock of children.

"Why, come on in, Tom! Did Ida have the baby?" came Mrs. Riley's brogue from the living room.

Hazel's heart beat wildly as she waited for her father's answer. "Yes, Mrs. Riley, and Ida's fine! Doc says the boy is a healthy specimen."

A boy! What a commotion followed as all the youngsters chattered at once! Hazel had a baby brother.

"Just like me!" Joey said proudly.

"Dad!" Hazel raced to his side. "May I see him? May I see my new brother?"

"Sure, Hazel! Come on!" Then Mr. Weston turned and thanked the housekeeper for "minding the girl."

"No bother, Tom! She was a perfect angel... Tell Ida I'll be over later with some of my good Irish stew for her. Best thing to help a new mother regain her strength."

"She'll appreciate that," Father replied as he and Hazel left. They crossed the orchard, hand in hand.

"What did you name him, Daddy?"

"Well, that was a problem, Young Lady. Your mother and Grandma and I have been considering names for quite some time. We finally decided on *Kelly*."

"Kelly! Kelly Weston!" Hazel repeated the name a few more times, then exclaimed, "I like it!"

Upon their arrival home, Grandma Smith greeted the girl. "You may go into your mother's room, Hazel. But you must be very quiet. The baby's sleeping."

"Yes, Ma'am," Hazel whispered, then tiptoed across to the room where her baby brother lay nestled in Mother's arm. His face, red and wrinkled, stuck out for her to admire.

Hazel bent down and peered at the baby. "Mom!" she whispered excitedly. "What's the matter with him? He's terribly red."

Mother looked amused. "As I recall, you were pretty red when you were first born also. In no time, though, you turned a healthy pink and your skin smoothed out."

The baby squirmed and opened his eyes, looking directly at his big sister.

"Oh, I'm sorry Kelly! I wasn't supposed to wake you."

Hazel felt Grandma tugging gently at her shoulder. "Come on, Child! Let's let your mother rest."

Hazel studied her baby brother a few more seconds, then turned to leave.

Later, alone in her room, she pondered over this new situation. She had been an only child for almost ten years. Now she would be sharing her parents and Grandma with Baby Kelly. What would that be like? Many questions sifted through her young mind that afternoon — questions that only time would answer.

VIII
BILLY FOUGHT

The kitchen, humming with activity, had held the strong, sweet fragrance of peaches since early morning, when the valley lay still and untouched by August's sun.

Now the room grew hotter by the minute as a symphony of banging pans and boiling water filled Hazel's ears.

The smothering heat made sweat trickle down the girl's face and throat. She took little comfort in the cool water running over her fingers and the peaches she peeled for canning.

"Why can't fruit grow in the winter when it's cold?" she asked herself. "Then I'd welcome this heat."

The more she peeled fruit, the more she fretted. Pears would ripen next, then late peaches, then apples. Hazel felt overwhelmed by the thought of bushel upon bushel of fruit yet to be canned and stored in the cellar.

"Lucky for us we have Grandma," she consoled herself. Then she turned her thoughts to the new baby Mother was feeding in the dining room. "That Kelly makes more work for everybody. So many diapers to wash — and clothes! He must get his outfit changed at least ten times a day!"

The girl's disgruntled face made Grandma ask, "What's eating you, Girl? Cut your finger or something?"

"No! I was just thinking about all the extra work now that Kelly's here. We even have to put up more peaches because of him."

"Why, I'm surprised at you, Hazel! Don't you love that little fellow anymore?"

"Y — yes! It's just ... well ... this is supposed to be my vacation, and it isn't a vacation at all."

A smile crinkled Grandma's face. "Hazel, have I ever told you about your Aunt Maggie, the teamdriver?"

"Nooo!" The girl brightened.

"Let me tell you about her then," Grandma declared as she lowered a new batch of jars into the kettle. "Threshing time had come, and Emery thought he'd be smart and hire a genuine teamster from town. But before long he realized the fellow was a poor driver. In fact, he was so bad that he made Emery's good workhorses start balding under the collar."

Hazel frowned. She knew that all her uncle's horses were as dear to him as if they were his own children.

"Well," continued Grandma, "Emery came into the kitchen where Maggie and a hired lady were preparing dinner for the threshing crew. 'Maggie!' he hollered, 'You've got to drive the team for me. That fellow from town doesn't know a horse from a wheelbarrow! And I sent him packing.' "

"What did Aunt Maggie say to that, Grandma?"

"Nothing, Child! She simply checked the boiling potatoes and then followed her husband out to the fields." The old woman peered deep into Hazel's eyes. "And do you know what? Maggie not only drove the team the whole day long, she also managed to feed all those threshers, tidy the house, and keep the chickens out of the garden."

"Whew!" Hazel sighed. Looking over at the several boxes of fruit waiting in the corner, she said, "Maybe I don't have so much to do after all!"

Grandma chuckled and said no more.

With Mother's help, the remaining peaches were canned by three o'clock that afternoon. Hazel wiped her damp brow and collapsed onto a nearby chair.

"Don't get too comfortable!" her mother warned. I've got just enough time before supper to measure the hems of your new school dresses."

Hazel dragged her tired feet into the dining room where she climbed atop a stool.

As Mother tucked under the first hem, she declared, "Hazel, I do believe you've grown several inches since last year at this time."

Grandma piped up. "I told you she would grow, Ida, as soon as those old tonsils were out."

Hazel beamed. She was growing — finally!

September arrived, and the schoolhouse at Barrett filled up with children again. Hazel no longer occupied the overflow room, but became a member of the fifth-sixth grade class. Miss Knowles was her new teacher.

Hazel spent her lunch hour the first day of school, catching up on the summer's news with Holly and Margie.

When most of the fruit was finally harvested, autumn's chill settled over the valley. It was then that Mr. Weston brought home an unusual visitor to stay for the winter.

Hazel couldn't help staring at the ancient-looking cowboy who stalked into the house. He could easily have popped out of an old-West storybook. Even his name sounded fictitious — Billy Fought. Tanned, leathery skin, mapped with wrinkles, showed a lifetime of hard work outdoors. He had a sweeping, handlebar mustache. And to top off Billy's tall, lanky frame, a ten-gallon hat perched atop his head.

"Yep!" Father declared. "Billy and I go back a long way. He used to be roundup cook for us Imnaha cowpunchers. He's going to set up his tent in our back yard for a spell."

"There's plenty of room in the house, Mr. Fought," Mother said.

"No, no, Ma'am!" the old cowboy protested. "I'll be fine in my tent. Just as long as I have lots of books and my little stove, I'll be fine." Then he strode out to where he and Father set up his makeshift home for winter.

"Brrr!" Hazel thought. "How can he stand living outside in the cold?"

89

terryharper 83

Grandma read the girl's expression. "That tent can stay pretty warm, Hazel, and it's much better than sleeping in a bedroll under the stars, which he's probably done most of his life. To Billy Fought, that tent is a palace."

The girl still looked doubtful. How could a tent ever be any kind of a home for long?

After days of observing the old cowpuncher, however, Hazel began to understand. Billy Fought would come in for meals, reminisce with Father about "the good ol' days," then seem drawn back to his tent.

"I guess home is anyplace a person feels comfortable and contented," Hazel concluded to herself.

Once Father cautioned the old man, "You'd better be careful about cranking that stove up so high, Billy. It could cause trouble, you know."

A slow grin spread across the old face. That was the cowboy's only response.

Little Kelly grew more lively by the day. He would lie on the living-room couch and set his small arms and legs in motion, like a miniature steam engine chugging away.

One afternoon Billy Fought ambled over to the baby, who was again "spinning his wheels." The cowboy laughed at the sight, then hollered, "Go to it, Boy!" But little Kelly still went nowhere.

As winter approached, Mother kept her promise and allowed Holly to spend the night with Hazel.

It was a lazy, Sunday afternoon, and except for occasional gurgling sounds from Kelly, the house was quiet. Father relaxed in his favorite chair, seemingly paying no attention to Hazel and Holly across the room.

For want of a better pastime, the girls decided to play Hide-the-Thimble. Kelly watched their every move from his spectator's spot on the couch, while Father hid behind his newspaper.

Finally Mr. Weston asked, "Mind if I hide the thimble this time?"

The question startled Hazel. Her father, always businesslike, never played games.

"I guess so," she replied.

The two girls shut their eyes until Father called, "Ready!"

Holly and Hazel began their search. They combed every inch of the living room and dining room, but couldn't find the thimble anywhere. Hazel was ready to give up in exasperation when the light caught a glint of silver — of all the places — atop her father's bald head!

"Oh, Daddy!" she cried with glee. "That was the best hiding place ever!"

Holly's wish was granted at last when Grandma Smith told her some stories that evening. Hazel had heard them several times over, but never tired of the tales.

Afterward, when the girls were tucked into the little brass bed, Holly sighed. "Hazel, your grandmother is everything you said she was. What exciting stories!"

A feeling of pride swept through Hazel. "Yes, and do you know I want to become a nurse just like her someday?"

"You don't say?" Holly sounded excited. "I want to be a nurse too."

Hazel changed the subject. "You know, it's almost Thanksgiving time again, and we haven't had any snow yet."

"I'm glad," Holly said. "Last year we almost lost my mother."

"I remember . . . Holly, what's it like? I mean, how do you feel about your mother always being so sick? You don't talk much about it anymore."

Holly's quiet voice penetrated the still, dark room. "I've never told you about Mamma's special talk, have I?"

"No!"

"Well," Holly began, "last winter after she made it through that worst spell, Mamma drew me close to her and said some wonderful things. She told me that many mothers are allowed to watch their children grow up and get married, but the mothers never really appreciate the children. And even if they do, many times they leave unsaid the things they feel in their hearts, and their children grow up never knowing their mother's true feelings at all." Holly paused and took a deep breath.

"Mamma said that although she probably never will live to see me march down the aisle, that our few years together are like fine gold. Each morning she wakes up she thanks God that she's alive another day, and she promises Him that she'll make the most of every minute."

Hazel peered out at the blackness as Holly's words sifted softly into her young heart.

The girl continued, "Mamma showed me a verse in the Bible that says, 'Teach us to number our days, that we may apply our hearts unto wisdom.' I'll never forget that verse, Hazel. Mamma lives it every day. If she thinks of something good about one of her children, she tells us. She loves us, and we know it."

Tears swelled out of Hazel's eyes, but she steadied her voice so Holly wouldn't know she was crying. "Don't you feel sad that she won't be able to see you grow up?"

"Sometimes, Hazel. But when I think about that verse and about what Mamma said, I feel better. Anyway, all the things she's taught me will live on and on, long after she's gone."

Holly's voice trailed off into the soft breathing of slumber. Hazel, however, lay awake a long while, pondering serious questions: Did she fully appreciate her own mother? What about Dad and Grandma? How often did she fail to tell them how she felt about them? As she pulled the quilt up higher, she vowed to let them know at least once a day how much they meant to her. If only through her actions, she would tell them. After all, her grandmother had told her many times, "actions speak louder than words."

Thanksgiving came and went, and Hazel did her best to keep her promise. She helped everywhere she could and hugged Baby Kelly often.

On Christmas morning Mother tiptoed into her room. "Hazel, you've been such a good girl this past month. I've brought you a Christmas present." Mother placed a large, green book in the girl's hands. The book, *UNCLE BEN'S CLOVERFIELD,* was the sequel to last year's present.

Hazel beamed. "Thank you, Mom! I can't wait to read it." Suddenly, Holly's words came to mind, and Hazel deliberately kissed her mother, exclaiming, "I love you, Mom!"

Mrs. Weston blinked in surprise, then left her daughter to read the new book.

Within the pages Hazel met Little Gracie and Tom, and again found the nature stories delightful. This book opened a whole new world to the girl. It planted a yearning within her, a yearning to know more about the God who created the miraculous little hummingbird she read about in one of the stories.

Hazel wondered about her father. Why did he seem so against religion? She knew her mother and grandmother read their Bibles regularly, but never attended a church. Nor did they speak about their faith in front of Father.

While she thought about these questions that cold, winter morning, a loud boom rocked the house. Then she heard Billy Fought's voice, "Yeeeiii!"

Springing to the window, Hazel froze at the sight. Smoke barrelled out of Billy's tent while the man jumped around the yard, screeching and holding scorched hands to his face.

IX
TO NUMBER OUR DAYS

Hazel darted out the back door after her parents. Without a moment's hesitation, Father grabbed a shovel and hurled snow at the burning tent while Mother led the injured cowboy back to the house.

Tagging behind them, Hazel felt her heart pounding furiously. "Poor Billy!" she thought, keeping her head down, afraid to look at his burned face.

When she did look, the girl cringed at the sight. Sooty black patches covered the cowboy's blistering skin, and his once-magnificnet mustache had become a tangle of singed hair. Billy kept his eyes squinted shut, his mouth taut, saying nothing.

Grandma came to his aid at once with cold, damp cloths for his eyes. "Hold these here while Tom takes you down to Doc Wiley. He'll fix you up!" she said with a deliberate lilt to her voice.

In minutes Dad was leading the gray-haired man to the car. As soon as they were out of earshot, Grandma declared, "It's a wonder that stove didn't explode sooner, the way he kept it cranked up so high! Tom warned him."

"Do you think he'll go blind?" Mother asked anxiously.

"Can't tell, Ida! Don't worry about him, though. I'm sure that cowpuncher has been through worse than this."

"But his eyes, Mom. Reading is all he has left. His only family is a sister over at Maryhill. And he doesn't want to impose on her. In fact, that's why he's here this winter."

"I know, Ida," Grandma looked sympathetic. "But you're underestimating that man. He's tougher than a cow's hide. You'll see!"

When Dad returned later with Billy, he put the old man to bed on the living-room couch, but not without a struggle.

"I'll be fine," Billy insisted, his eyes still locked shut. "Just let me go back to my tent!"

"Don't be so stubborn!" Grandma scolded. "Out there you'd get those burns infected — if you didn't freeze to death first! Now, just lie down on that couch, and don't give us any backtalk!"

Billy mumbled something, but did as Grandma ordered.

He would see again, Doc Wiley had said. And after a month under the doctor's care — and Grandma's — Billy was free to go on his way, across the Columbia River to Maryhill, where he would "impose" on his sister again.

"Jest give me some pan drippin's and some beans, and I'll rustle up a meal anywhere!" the man drawled as he left the house. That was Billy's way of saying goodbye.

Easterly winds scoured the valley throughout February. Still, the weather seemed tame compared to the winter before. In March, chinooks blew from the Pacific and warmed the earth, drawing the first signs of spring around the valley.

Mother commented, "We'll be needing a cow soon, Tom. Kelly's getting to be a pretty big boy."

"I think I've done enough pruning to afford a good cow," Father said. "I'll see what I can find."

Then, as new grass sprouted everywhere, Father brought home Daisy, a pure white Jersey, as white as the milk she gave.

"You're beautiful!" Hazel exclaimed. Daisy rolled her soft brown eyes at the girl, seemingly unimpressed by the compliment.

It became Hazel's job each morning to water Daisy, then stake her out in the pasture behind the house. And as spring painted the valley with new leaves and buds, Hazel's chore became more pleasant each day.

One sunny April morning, Hazel dawdled on her way to the barn. Birds twittered overhead, while the sweet fragrance of grass permeated the air. Spring's enchantment seemed to fill the girl from her toes up until she felt light enough to flutter around like a butterfly.

"Good morning, Daisy!" Hazel called to the good-natured cow awaiting her morning drink.

In no time Hazel was skipping ahead of Daisy, looking for good grazing ground. She found a large patch of clover and pounded the cow's stake into the center of the patch.

"There! You'll have more than enough to eat until I return from school," the girl exclaimed. Then she hurried to the house, picked up her books, and ran out to the road just in time to meet the bus.

She didn't care that Nicky Cotton had already secured the front seat. The day was too warm and inviting, and anyway, she wanted to tell Holly about the wonderful patch of clover she had found.

When Hazel met the sober face of her friend, however, she knew there would be no talk of clover. Doctor Wiley's car at Holly's house told the story.

"Your mother's bad again?"

"Yes, Hazel. Quite bad!" The blond-haired girl's voice trembled. "Mamma wants to see the blossoms one more time, Hazel. Just one more time..."

"She will, Holly! I know she will!" Hazel tried to sound convincing.

That afternoon, on their walk home from school, the two girls cut across a field of high grass. Unexpectedly, they came upon a pheasant warming her nest. The startled bird flew up into their faces, and during the commotion she knocked many of her eggs down an embankment where they smashed against rocks.

"Oh, how dreadful!" Holly cried.

"I feel like a murderer," groaned Hazel.

On that gloomy note, the girls parted, but Hazel carried with her the awful sight of those eggs, crushed and ruined.

When she neared her back yard, she noticed that Daisy was sprawled on her side. "How strange!" Hazel thought, hurrying closer for a better look.

Daisy's eyes, glazed and staring, seemed empty. Her stomach bulged balloonlike against the ground. And the only sound Hazel heard was the buzzing of flies clustered about the cow's face.

"Mom!" the girl screamed, racing toward the back door. "Something's wrong with Daisy."

Mother appeared at once, then ordered the girl inside. Minutes later the woman returned, tearful. Hazel was dumbstruck. She had never seen her mother cry.

"Hazel, Daisy is dead."

"Dead?"

"The clover patch, Girl! You don't stake out a cow in clover! It causes bloat until the poor animal can't breathe." Mother choked out the words then headed for her room where she could hide her tears.

A blush of shame spread over the girl's face, and her voice came out strange and squeaky. "But I didn't know. No one ever told me that!"

"You're right, Girl!" Grandma consoled her. "How were you to know? Your mother just feels bad because your dad spent most of his pruning money to buy that cow. And Daisy *was* a beautiful animal — a good milker too!"

With that, Grandma bustled off to the kitchen and left Hazel in the empty room, alone with her thoughts. Indeed, she *was* a murderer. First those pheasant eggs, and now poor, poor Daisy!

She fled out the door and didn't stop running until she heard Harv Hodson's voice. "What's the matter, Hazel? You look like you've lost your best friend."

Hazel stopped alongside the boy's yard. "I have — almost. I killed Daisy, our cow. I staked her out in clover. Honestly, I didn't know what it would do to her."

Harv's face filled with sympathy for the girl. "I believe you."

Suddenly, Hazel remembered the book of Uncle Ben's nature stories and asked, "Harv, will Daisy be in Heaven someday?"

The boy hid a smile. "Well, I'm not sure about that, but I do know there'll be animals on the new Earth. Come on into the house! I'll show you."

The two youngsters entered the large living room, where the family Bible rested on a center table.

"We just had a sermon on this very subject," the boy said. "The text was Isaiah 11:6,7. Here, read it!"

Hazel read aloud:

"The wolf also shall dwell with the lamb,
and the leopard shall lie down with the kid;
and the calf and the young lion and the
fatling together; and a little child shall lead
them.

"And the cow and the bear shall feed;
their young ones shall lie down together:
and the lion shall eat straw like the ox."

Hazel clapped the Bible shut. "There *will* be cows in Heaven!" she cried out.

"Well, that's talking about the Earth made new, Hazel."

The girl looked puzzled. "When is all this going to happen?"

As Harv scratched his head, Mrs. Hodson came to his rescue. "Hello, Hazel! I couldn't help overhearing." The pretty woman sat down beside the girl. "Why don't you let the Bible answer your questions? Read I Thessalonians, 4:15 to 18!"

Harv breathed a sigh of relief while Hazel read to herself about how those who are alive when the Lord returns shall not go before those who are asleep. And when the Lord descends from Heaven, the dead in Christ will rise first.

Then she read aloud:

". . .we which are alive and remain shall
be caught up together with them in the

*clouds, to meet the Lord in the air: and so
shall we ever be with the Lord."*

"That's talking about the resurrection of the righteous, Hazel, the ones who have accepted Jesus as their Savior — or first resurrection. See, here in Revelation 20:6, it tells us more about it."

Hazel then read,

*"he that hath part in the first resurrection
. . .shall reign with (Christ) a thousand
years."*

"So that's when Christians go to Heaven, when Jesus comes back?" Hazel asked.

"Well, you read it yourself in Thessalonians, Hazel. Those who are asleep in Jesus will rise first, then —"

"Yes, I know." Hazel interrupted the woman. "But, Mrs. Hodson, why will Christians be in Heaven only a thousand years? What happens after that?"

The woman looked thoughtful. "We could get into the judgment of the wicked, but I don't think that's what you need right now. You'll find your answer in the next chapter of Revelation. Look at verses two and four!"

Hazel turned the page and read:

*"And I John saw the holy city, new
Jerusalem, coming down from God out of*

Heaven, prepared as a bride adorned for her husband. . .

"And God shall wipe away all tears from their eyes; and there shall be no more death, neither sorrow, nor crying, neither shall there be any more pain: for the former things are passed away."

"Oh, Mrs. Hodson! That's beautiful! May I read it again?" As Hazel reread the promises, her grief and anger slowly melted away. Then she closed the Bible and gently placed it back on the table.

"Thank you! I'm going home now," the girl announced, then skipped out the door, leaving two smiling Hodsons behind.

Hazel waited all evening for her father to mention the cow, but he never did. Because her mother seemed in brighter spirits, the girl decided not to bring up the subject herself.

A few weeks later, delicate white blooms puffed out all over the valley, nature's own lacework to dress up her orchards.

With the lovely blossoms all around them, Holly boarded the bus one sunny morning. She peeked around the canvas and waved to her mother.

"Mamma said this is surely the most beautiful spring she's ever seen," Holly remarked. "The blossoms look much fuller and fluffier."

Hazel agreed with her friend, then caught a glimpse of frail Mrs. Pennington gazing out her window. Indeed, the woman appeared to be drinking in the beauty all around her.

The girls sat near the back of the vehicle where they could enjoy the view as the bus drove through a blossom wonderland.

Everything went well that morning until Hazel overheard Miss Knowles whispering to Holly. "Your father's out in the hall. He'd like to see you."

Hazel held her breath while her friend walked with lagging steps toward the corridor. Then she heard Holly's muffled sobs. Hazel knew then that the dreaded time had come — Mrs. Pennington had finally given in to her illness.

Holly slipped back into the class and was heading for the cloakroom. Hazel followed her, and before she could ask, Holly blurted, ' 'She's gone!"

"I'm so sorry, Holly." Hazel's vision blurred with tears.

An awkward hush fell over the two girls, neither knowing what to say next until Hazel remarked, "Holly, she saw the blossoms!"

The blond-haired girl forced a smile. "You're right . . . and . . . and remember, she said they were the best she'd ever seen." Then Holly turned and

collected her sweater and lunchbucket. "Hazel, I'm afraid this is goodbye."

"What do you mean?"

"As soon as the funeral's over, Dad says we're moving up to Odell, now that we don't have to stay near town and the doctor anymore."

Hazel tried to make her voice sound cheerful. "Odel's not that far away, Holly. We'll meet again, I'm sure!"

"Maybe . . ."

Somewhere in the midst of her whirling thoughts, Hazel recalled, "Mr. Krause said your mom was a really good Christian. Do you know what that means?" Without giving Holly a chance to answer, Hazel rushed on, "A while ago, Mrs. Hodson shared some scriptures with me about Heaven and the new Jerusalem — you know, after Jesus comes back. The words were, 'and there shall be no more death, neither sorrow, nor crying, neither shall there be any more pain . . .' "

At first, Holly's blue eyes continued to stare into space as if she hadn't heard anything. Then a smile spread across her face. "You're right, Hazel. And Mom isn't suffering anymore, is she?"

"According to the Bible, your mother is 'asleep.' The next thing she'll realize, the Lord will be returning, and she'll see loved ones again."

Holly didn't say another word. She simply squeezed Hazel's hand and left.

That afternoon Hazel walked home alone. Only a short time ago her path had led through craggy, dead-looking trees, leafless and gray. Now spring's sun had brought the orchard to life, a rebirth of color and beauty.

New awareness for that life and beauty welled up within the girl as Mrs. Pennington's motto came back to her, *Teach us to number our days . . .*

X
LOST

Birds twittered "good night" from treetops as shadows crept across the valley. Hazel's yawn hinted of bedtime.

With summer approaching, days grew longer, and it seemed strange to the girl to go to bed before dark. But she did so willingly, because the busy final days of school always wearied her. Just seconds after climbing into bed, Hazel fell fast asleep.

The girl slept so soundly she never woke to a truck's roar outside her window. Neither did she hear some mysterious sounds by the barn.

When Hazel stirred again, it was morning, and she sensed at once that a secret was floating about the house. She looked from parent to parent, then to Grandma, but not a one let her in on their secret.

Suddenly, Father jumped up from the table and said, "When you're finished with breakfast, Hazel, come on out to the barn!"

Burning with curiosity, Hazel gulped down her food, then raced outside. Halting by the open barn door, she was astounded to see the gentle face of a large cow.

"So this is the big secret!" Hazel exclaimed, breathless. "What's her name, Daddy?"

"Daisy."

"Again?"

"Yep! The name seems popular for cows." Father's eyes twinkled as he continued, "Her coloring and size make her look like a Holstein, but she's supposed to be a Jersey, guaranteed to give us plenty of milk."

Daisy Number Two nuzzled the girl as if to say, "How do you do?"

Hazel studied the cow. In no way did she resemble her handsome predecessor. In fact, this Daisy was rather homely with her bulky size and gray markings.

Then Hazel noticed the large spot on the animal's right side — a perfectly shaped, three-leaf clover, a reminder of the other cow's awful death. And because of the girl's tragic mistake, Hazel guessed that her father probably would never trust her with this new cow.

Before the girl could ask, Father placed the rope in her hands, saying, "Here! You can go stake her out now."

Hazel's sober face grew radiant.

"He trusts me!" she thought, squaring her shoulders. "Come on, Daisy! I'll find you a nice, *safe* place to eat."

That afternoon Hazel skipped merrily home, singing all the way, "Only two more days of fifth grade, two more days of fifth grade."

"Howdy, Big Enough!" a familiar voice interrupted the girl's song.

Hazel looked up into the face of a grinning cowboy. "Uncle Roy!" she squealed delightedly. Then in the next breath, she asked, "Is Gink here too?"

"Nope! There's just me on my way home from a cattle sale in Portland." The man's thick, dark hair bobbed with each word. "But your cousin sends her regards, Big Enough." Uncle Roy laughed his jolly way, then stood back and surveyed his niece from head to toe. "I don't believe it, Gal. You're really growing — finally!"

Hazel looked at the ground, replying modestly, "It was my tonsils, Uncle Roy. Grandma said that once they were out I'd grow, and — I am!"

Uncle Roy leaned back in his boots and roared with laughter. "You don't say? Well, Mom's pretty smart. She must know what she's talking about."

At supper Uncle Roy recounted his trip by train to Portland and brought news from his Idaho ranch. "Sure am happy you folks live along the route. I've been wondering if this valley of yours was for real. I'll have to admit, it sure beats anything I've laid eyes on before."

Hazel glowed with pride for her valley.

Next, Mr. Weston reported on their winter and how the roof almost caved in.

Uncle Roy glanced upward, exclaiming, "Boy! You were sure lucky, Tom!"

Mother and Grandma smiled knowingly at each other, as if to say, "We don't call an answer to prayer, 'luck' "

As soon as Hazel dried the dishes, she joined her family by the stove. Uncle Roy always had a bagful of stories up his sleeve, and she was hoping for one.

The short man drawled, "Did I ever tell you about an old white horse I owned named Jay?"

Hazel leaned expectantly toward her uncle.

"That old mount was perfectly homely. I mean he was so ugly that it was a good thing he never looked at himself in a mirror, or he would have died of either fright or misery!"

Everyone laughed.

Uncle Roy continued, "Looks aren't everything, you know. Old Jay was perfect for roundups, because he never got tired.

Hazel knew that roundups meant long hours of backbreaking work.

The visitor went on, "We'd been out all day when I spotted a renegade steer. We'd tried to catch that fellow the season before, but he was always too quick and made a clean getaway."

Hazel nodded. She was aware that a renegade could do harm by leading other steers away from the herd.

"Well, when I spotted that guy just daring me to chase him, my blood boiled," Uncle Roy told them. "I shouted, and took out after him on ugly old Jay."

Hazel tried to imagine her slim, short uncle charging after the steer over the rough terrain in Idaho.

"That critter looked like he'd been shot out of a cannon," her Uncle said. "But old Jay kept right up with him — didn't even seem winded. Then just as we came upon a washout, the steer tore off to the right, and we kept going straight for that wide ditch. I knew I was a goner for sure. That washout was a jumble of sharp snags sticking up all over, like a bed of knives just waiting for me and my horse to land on."

Hazel gasped. She was so interested in the story that she forgot her uncle couldn't have died, because he was sitting in front of her.

The man's voice rose. "Then, with a great big jolt, Jay leaped into the air. I shut my eyes and clenched my teeth, waiting for my tortured end. To my surprise, I felt strangely light as a whooshing sounded in my ears. The next thing I knew, we had landed on the other side of the washout, right next to the steer who had taken a different route. I roped him good. Then after he settled down, I looked back at that ditch and shuddered. To this day, I don't know how that horse made it across — unless he sprouted wings. Jay might be ugly, but he's the *jumpinest* horse I've ever known!"

"And the moral of the story is that looks aren't everything," Hazel added.

"Right ya are, Big Enough!" Uncle Roy said.

Mother then reminded Hazel about bedtime, so the girl reluctantly left the group behind and trudged toward her room.

A smile played on her lips. Everybody else called her "Hazel" now. But Uncle Roy, who had nicknamed her years ago, still called her "Big Enough." She found herself liking the nickname — especially since she was growing at last.

Hazel's summer toil always made the hot months roll by at top speed, and before she realized it, school began again, and she was a sixth grader under the tutorage of Miss Holbrook.

Margie Phillips remained her best friend now that Holly had moved away. Occasionally, Lucy Trent palled around with Hazel, but for the most part, she and Margie were inseparable.

Autumn silently stole into the valley, taking with it the green finery of that year. And when winter arrived, the snow wasn't the threatening kind, but well packed and perfect for sledding.

One moonlit evening, Hazel was aroused by a commotion outside. Then Margie and Buddy Phillips appeared at her front door. Breathlessly, Margie asked, "Can you go for a ride on our double bob, Hazel? Noel's a good driver, you know."

Hazel turned questioningly to her mother.

"Go ahead!" the woman said. "Just bundle up well first!"

The girl scampered off to her room and put on all sorts of woolen clothes. In minutes she and Margie were climbing into the box on the bobsled.

The sweet smell of alfalfa filled the crisp air as Hazel settled down into the prickly hay.

Noel called, "Giddyup!" starting the horses down Belmont toward Hood River Heights. Some of the children began to sing, and Hazel joined them. Their voices rang out into the surrounding countryside, where snow-clad orchards glistened in the moonlight.

Just before spring's chinooks set in, they took another bobsled ride. Noel felt daring that evening and drove faster and faster until his brother shouted through the wind, "Noel, you'd better slow those horses, or they'll catch pneumonia!"

Noel didn't reply, but tugged gently on the reins, slowing the team to a walk for the rest of the evening.

As the sled turned back toward Hazel's house, Margie startled her friend with some sad news. "We're moving away."

The words pierced through Hazel like a stinging east wind. "Where? Why? When?" she blurted out.

"Not until school's over, but we're definitely moving. Dad's got a better offer in an orchard elsewhere. He said it won't be quite as much work as this place." Margie hung her head. "I'm sorry! I feel really bad about it."

Hazel sat quietly thinking. "First, I lose Holly — now Margie." Then she remembered what Mrs. Pennington had said about appreciating her loved ones.

"Well, we'll just have to make your remaining days here the best ever!" Hazel said determinedly.

"Yes!" the other girl exclaimed. "We will do just that!"

The pale moonlight revealed two grinning faces.

From then on the girls used every opportunity to be together, whether riding the bus or walking home from school. But the days sped by too fast, and soon their sixth year of school was drawing to a close.

Then one warm May afternoon, Hazel found a tearful Margie at her door. "It's my little brother, Joey!" the girl cried. "He's disappeared. Most of our neighbors have joined the search, and if we don't find him soon, Dad's going to call the police."

Hazel was speechless. Little Joey — gone?

Mr. Weston had overheard. "Come on, Hazel!" he said, while patting Margie's back reassuringly. "Don't worry! We'll find your brother."

As their swift steps brought the threesome through the orchard toward Alameda Road, Margie panted, "He's just a little fellow, only five years old. Oh, Hazel! What if he's hiked down to the Columbia River and fallen in?"

Hazel looked indignant. "Stop that silly talk! Joey could never walk that far." But all the while she was thinking of the pond across from the Phillips place. Could the swimming hole have become a death trap for the boy?

Margie answered her silent question. "They checked the pond first thing and didn't find a sign of anyone's being there recently. Oh, I love that little guy so much!"

Hazel felt a few hot tears spilling down her cheeks as she thought of her own little brother. Kelly, just two, was now toddling everywhere, always grinning and saying new words with each day.

"The whole thing started with Mrs. Riley, when she spanked Joey because he'd been naughty," Margie explained. "Next thing the housekeeper knew, he was gone."

Father reached the house before the girls did. Other people milled around, then divided into groups to search the alfalfa fields and the orchards in a systematic way.

"There are over twenty-five acres to this farm," Mr. Phillips told them, his brow wrinkled with worry.

Hazel joined Margie in walking back and forth through apple trees and in checking their leafy limbs for the missing boy. Downed blossoms lay like snow under the fruit trees, but no one noticed their beauty that day. Once more Hazel's dream valley had turned into a villain. Now it seemed to be trying to claim little Joey's life, little Joey with the bright red hair and perpetually dirty face that smiled and frowned all at once.

The girls talked little to each other. They saved their voices for calling the boy. Hazel walked and walked until she thought her feet would fall off. Finally, as dusk crept over the orchards, they rejoined the others back at the house.

Mr. Phillisp shook his head. "I'm sure we've covered this ranch several times over, and there's no sign of him anywhere."

Hazel heard her father's husky voice, "What about the barn? Did you check the barn?"

"Twice!" Noel answered.

Suddenly, Hazel got an overwhelming urge to check the barn again — the same barn where she had been trapped. So the girl slipped quietly away from the group and headed toward the barn. Not a thing stirred in the blackness within the massive building. Hazel swallowed hard, thinking about bats and other night creatures that might be lurking in there.

Then she noticed the shed attached to the barn. The shed acted as a garage for the Phillips car. "I'll check there first," she decided, gladly leaving the eerie barn for the moment.

Low murmuring from the yard drifted to her in the stillness. Hazel heard the word "police" several times as she squeezed between the car and the shed's wall. It was so dark she could barely see the empty front seat of the car. Eager to leave the shed, she turned to go, then hesitated. "I might as well check the back seat while I'm here," she sighed.

Moments later she spotted the little clump that was Joey, sound asleep in the back of the car. Hazel rubbed her eyes in disbelief, then raced back to the yard.

"I've found him! It's Joey!"

Such a commotion followed! Voices, lanterns, Margie's grateful face, all became a blur. Finally, Mr. Phillips lifted the boy. "If I wasn't so happy to find you alive, Son, I'd really spank you!"

Joey sniffed. "Mrs. Riley already spanked me."

The crowd roared with amusement — and relief.

Mr. Weston took hold of his daughter's hand and led the way home. "Well, Girl, it looks like we have a real hero in the family."

Hazel's face glowed. Then, without warning, her spirits plunged to their lowest depths when she remembered that in a few short days, the Phillips family would leave Alameda Road. She would miss her best friend, Margie, and her mischievous little brother.

She wondered about the new people who would move into their house. Whoever they were, Hazel knew they could never take the Phillips's place in her heart.

XI
SANTA CLAUS IN MAY

The last day of school meant the last walk with Margie and the last wave goodbye. Hazel watched her friend disappear into the thick foliage that dressed the orchard.

She refused to cry. After all, she would soon be a seventh grader.

Arriving home, Hazel found the next-door neighbor, Mrs. Thompson, in her living room.

The woman was bubbling with excitement. "Hazel, I just asked your mother if you'd like to go with me to Sunday school and church this weekend, or all summer if you want. We'd be walking the three miles — "

The girl didn't hesitate. "Oh, yes!" she interrupted, forgetting her manners. Then she turned to her mother. "What about Dad? Do you think he'd let me go?"

"I'm not sure, Hazel. But I'll ask him tonight after supper." Just then Kelly awoke from his nap and Mother excused herself.

Mrs. Thompson headed for the door. "I'll pray that your dad will let you go with me. The weather's perfect for walking this time of year, and it would be nice to have your company. And, Hazel, you'd enjoy your Sunday school teacher. She's really good."

A mixture of smiles and frowns, Hazel wondered about her father. Would he let her go with Mrs. Thompson?

As soon as supper was over, the girl quickly cleared the table, leaving her parents alone. While washing dishes, Hazel strained to hear bits of conversation from the dining room.

"Tom, Hazel will turn twelve in July," came Mother's voice. "Her girlhood's nearly over. Let her enjoy being a child for a while! After all, every summer means nothing but work for her. What does she have to look forward to anyway?"

"Work never hurt anybody," Dad's husky voice returned. "Why, when I was a boy — "

Grandma splashed silverware into the soapy dishwater. "We'll have these done in no time," she said.

"Uh-huh," Hazel replied.

Again Mother's voice filtered into the kitchen, "It would be just for the summer. Mrs. Thompson needs company on her walk."

"Oh, all right!" boomed Father. "Just for the summer then! But, Ida, I don't want this church stuff to turn into a regular thing."

Grandma's merry eyes met Hazel's. "Well, Girl, it looks like you'll be going to the Baptist church with Mrs. Thompson."

Hazel grinned. Her grandmother had been listening all the time too.

Finishing her task, the girl became wrapped in deep thought. She wondered why her father seemed so against religion. Maybe a strong, self-sufficient person like him considered faith a sign of weakness, although he did respect Butch Krause, a lay preacher. . .

In a few days, Hazel was elbow-deep in canning again. But her chores didn't seem quite as toilsome, because all week she looked forward to Sunday morning when she and Mrs. Thompson would walk the three miles to Pine Street. There, a sturdy white church waited to fill up with people.

For those two hours a week, a new world opened to Hazel, one made up of rousing hymns, joyful voices, and best of all — Bible study. That Book — so long a mystery to her — was coming to life.

"No wonder Mom and Grandma like to read their Bibles!" Hazel thought. Those Sunday hours never lasted long enough for her.

The vacant Phillips house had looked forlorn until the new occupants moved in. But Hazel was disappointed when she met the Welton children, too young for her to do things with. Billy Welton was eight years old, while his sisters, Susie and Haddie, were only six and four. They looked like three stairsteps when they stood together.

An August sun blazed high above Hazel as she strolled along with Mrs. Thompson one Sunday afternoon. Sadly, the girl realized that summer would soon be over, ending the enjoyable excursions with her neighbor.

Just after Hazel sat down to lunch, Butch Krause rapped on the door.

"Come in and join us, Mr. Krause!" Mother said. "We have plenty."

"No, thank you, Mrs. Weston! I just wanted you to know about the Welton children, so you could go over later and check on the family. I'm tied up for the rest of the day, but I might be able to drop by tomorrow morning."

Hazel put down her fork and listened intently.

"What do you mean, Butch?" Father asked. "Have those youngsters gotten into some kind of mischief already?"

"The worst kind, Tom! You know the pond this side of Alameda Road?"

"Yes."

A terrible dread overwhelmed Hazel. She remembered suspecting the pond when Joey Phillips disappeared.

"You see," Mr. Krause explained, "I was on my way home from the Beasley place after church, when I came across Cliff Welton running like a madman toward the pond. From the look on his face, I decided to pull over and follow him."

It was then that Hazel noticed Mr. Krause's suit was mud-spattered.

The visitor went on, "I could hear a dog barking wildly down by the pond. As we were running Cliff said he'd heard Billy holler a few times. And when the dog started raising such a fuss, he feared the worst. Although his children had been ordered never to cross the road, apparently Billy at least had disobeyed him."

Hazel forgot all about lunch and kept her eyes fixed on the large man as he continued his story.

"When we reached the pond, my heart stopped beating. There was Tip, their dog, barking frantically. Then he'd stop the racket long enough to tug at Billy, who was standing at the pond's edge. Then Tip would bark some more. Young Billy looked as white as a sheet, holding tight to his sister's hand. But the heads of both girls were under water! I thought surely they were goners. We pulled them out and gave them artificial respiration. After we pumped some water out of their lungs, they started breathing." The man let out a sigh of relief. "I've never prayed so hard in all my life!"

Grandma asked, "Will the girls be all right?"

"That's why I'm here, Mrs. Smith. I helped Cliff haul them back up to his car, and he took them to the hospital. They were just barely conscious. I thought you might like to check with him later and see how they're doing. And I would appreciate it if you'd mention I'll be by in the morning."

"We will," Mom promised as Mr. Krause rose to leave.

Hazel ate the rest of her dinner in silence. She kept thinking over and over, "If Tip hadn't barked so much, those little girls probably would have drowned."

Later on, her parents brought news that the Welton household was back in order. Also, the three youngsters would never again cross Alameda Road without asking. They had learned their lesson.

A bright September morning marked the beginning of school. Mrs. Yarroll would double as the principal and the seventh-eighth grade teacher. Hazel thought that a person with such an important position would be tall and stern, but that didn't describe Mrs. Yarroll at all. Resembling a penguin, the short roundish woman wore her black hair rolled up in a knot atop her head. And the teacher possessed a great deal of spunk — as the children discovered the next day.

When Hazel arrived with her friend, Lucy Trent, at the schoolhouse, they were surprised by what looked like a circus act in progress. A crowd of young spectators had gathered, cheering boisterously as they watched two boys climb straight up the tall building.

"They're trying for the bell tower," explained an onlooker.

"Oh, no!" Hazel wailed. "If they should fall, they'd break their necks! Why are they doing such a stunt?"

"You know Ed Callahan," Lucy retorted. "He does anything for a laugh. It's too bad his little brother, Brian, is following his example."

Hazel thought that Ed was a likable fellow — mischievous at times, but likable.

Anyone could tell that he and Brian were brothers from their many freckles and their bright-orange hair. Now the two boys were gingerly climbing up, up the corner bricks, nearing the bell tower.

Without warning, Mrs. Yarroll appeared from nowhere. "Ed and Brian Callahan! You get yourselves down here this instant!" she ordered, her face glaring under the black topknot.

Ed called down, "Don't worry, Teacher! We'll climb in through the window on the top floor."

"Aw, Ed!" complained Brian. "I really wanted to make it to the bell tower!"

With those words, Mrs. Yarroll turned purple and raced back into the building. A few minutes later Hazel spotted a long, hairy arm reaching out of the third-story window and "helping" Ed inside.

"Must be the janitor!" guessed Harv Hodson, grinning. "I wouldn't want to be in the shoes of those fellows at this moment!"

Again the mysterious arm reached out and collared Brian, until he too was safely inside. Then

Mrs. Yarroll appeared and called down in a sugar-sweet voice, "Ten more minutes of recess! Have fun!"

Hazel didn't know what happened upstairs, but later she noticed the two Callahans were not at all their usual, clowning selves.

The rest of the day passed uneventfully until Hazel remembered that Edith Hodson had promised her part of a rose bush that afternoon. "That thing is spreading like wildfire," Edith had explained. "I'll be glad to share it with you."

So as soon as Hazel changed her clothes, she went directly over to Hodsons where Edith was already at work with a shovel.

"Now where did I lay my gloves?" the older girl murmured, then whirled around. "Eugene!" she called to her little brother. "Did you take my gloves?"

A smirking three-year-old rounded the corner of the house. He dangled his sister's work gloves playfully in front of her nose, then turned and scampered off.

"You rascal!" Edith raced after the boy. "That's the third time you've teased me. If you don't quit, I'm going to give you back to the Indians!" she threatened.

At once Eugene turned into a perfect gentleman, watching his sister's every move. Then, as she bent over to tug at a stubborn root, the lad gave her a deliberate shove. Down she went, headlong into a dirt pile.

At that moment, Hazel heard a clopping sound. Eugene had heard it too, because his eyes bulged with fright. As coincidence would have it, a wagonload of *Indians* was coming up the road.

The boy squealed and squirmed as Edith marched him toward the horse-drawn wagon, waving her free arm to stop the Indians.

Two long-haired men sat in front of two plump squaws, while children, dark and staring, were heaped everywhere in between. The wagon slowed to a stop in front of Edith and her squirming little brother.

A hush fell over all of them until Edith spoke up in a businesslike voice to one of the men. "I was wondering, Sir, if you would like another papoose? This one is a real pest, and I've run out of patience with him."

Eugene's eyes grew so wide that Hazel thought they would pop out as the boy stared up into the stern Indian faces.

Without a trace of emotion, the man looked Eugene over, then nodded, and motioned with his thumb to put the boy in the back.

Eugene squealed again, then jerked loose, and disappeared around the corner of the house. Hazel and Edith burst into laughter. The old Indian, however, just sighed loudly and started his team into motion. Not even the children smiled as they passed.

"Well, Hazel," Edith cried, "that'll be the last time Eugene tries to trick me!"

Hazel agreed as she happily took her rose bush home to plant on the west side of the house. From then on, every time she gazed upon the lovely yellow flowers that bloomed yearly, she would remember Eugene and the Indians.

That winter Hazel felt keenly the loss of Margie Phillips and her family. She missed the bobsled rides — the evenings that had bubbled over with singing, the beauty of winter, and the cozy warmth that only friendship brings.

With spring came the excitement of plannning the annual program for the seventh-eighth grade class. Since their school had no auditorium, all assemblies were held at Rockford Grange Hall.

Programs called for practice, and practice meant getting out of Friday afternoon study time — that is, for everyone except Hazel Weston and Ed Callahan.

The girl explained her sad situation to Lucy, "You see, my father would have to commit himself in saying that he'd definitely be available to take me to the program that night. And Dad never could promise that." Hazel sighed. "He'll most probably be there, but to say he *definitely* will be there is dishonest in his book. So I'll have to stay here with Ed. His folks feel the same way my dad does."

Lucy groaned. "You mean, you won't be able to take part in the program at all?"

"Not as long as Dad won't commit himself," Hazel replied sadly.

As a result, on Friday afternoon Hazel and Ed watched somberly from their desks as their classmates left for their walk to the Rockford Grange Hall.

Mrs. Yarroll stayed behind with the two glum students. "Well, Ed, this would be a good time for you to catch up on your geography lesson."

Hazel hoped that Mrs. Yarroll would tell her the same thing. She loved geography. An afternoon spent browsing through *NATIONAL GEOGRAPHICS* would be great.

"And, Hazel," the teacher broke into her day-dreaming, "I think you should brush up on your spelling. Final exams will be here in no time."

"Yes, Ma'am," Hazel replied, dissappointment dripping from her voice.

But the afternoon took a turn for the better when a knock sounded at the door. In hobbled an ancient man with waist-length, wooly white whiskers. Hazel thought he was the perfect picture of Santa Claus, except for his slender frame.

"Mrs. Yarroll, I presume?" The quavering voice added mystery to the man. I'm Adam Fry, the first teacher Barrett ever had, way back when the school was just a log building."

"How interesting!" Mrs. Yarroll said.

Ed's dancing eyes glanced over at Hazel as if to say, "Look what the others are missing!"

Mrs. Yarroll explained to the oldtimer the absence of most of her class.

The man's eyes sparkled kindly. "It looks like you poor youngsters got the bad part of the deal. H'mmmm!" He rubbed his bristly chin. "I'd like to share a bit of history with you two — that is, with the teacher's permission, of course!"

"Go right ahead, Mr. Fry!" the woman replied graciously.

The man opened his story. "When I taught at Barrett, I was only seventeen and had my hands full with some of the livelier students — especially one little lad named Johnny. He was forever teasing the girls. So I had to make him stay in during many a recess."

138

Hazel looked over at Ed and thought how much like Johnny he was — he and his pranks!

The bearded man continued, "First, let me explain about the schoolhouse. As I said, it was a log building, two-storied. Now, the first story formed an open shed where we kept the wood for the stove. The schoolroom floor upstairs had been laid green. When those boards shrunk, they left gaping cracks." He chuckled. "Those cracks came in quite handy after lunch. All we needed to do was sweep all the crumbs through the floor and into the wood pile below. An excellent setup!"

Hazel and Ed laughed.

Making his way to the window, Mr. Fry looked toward the road. "The schoolhouse was over in that direction. Anyway, getting back to Johnny — after one of his usual escapades, I made him stay in after lunch. Back then we didn't have fancy desks like you have here. The children sat on long benches that stretched the width of the classroom. One long plank served as desks for each row. Well, Johnny had seated himself and was supposedly studying, his face hidden behind a book, when he started to scoot across the bench. Back and forth he traveled, keeping his head downward and buried in that book."

A sly expression crossed the man's face as he remembered the incident. "I wasn't much more than a boy myself, you know, so I suspected something was up. I tiptoed behind him, but didn't notice anything peculiar. Finally, I couldn't stand the suspense any longer. 'Young Man!' I barked. 'What *are* you doing?"

" 'Shhh, Teacher!' said he. 'You'll scare 'em!'

" 'Scare what?' I asked indignantly.

" 'Why, the quail!' said Johnny. And sure enough! Looking down through the cracks, I spotted a mother quail and her many babies scattered throughout the wood pile. They were enjoying a banquet on our leftover crumbs!"

Mr. Fry paused a moment, seemingly pleased with Hazel's broad smile. "So, instead of his geography, Johnny had a good nature lesson!" laughed the old man. "Yes, sometimes it's better to stay behind."

Mrs. Yarroll spoke up, "May I ask where you went after Barrett?"

"Yes. This country was getting civilized with lots of farms starting up. I decided to homestead up in Alaska, and have been teaching in little schoolhouses up there ever since."

Hazel's eyes filled with admiration for the old gentleman. He was a true pioneer, just like Grandma Smith had been. She couldn't wait to tell Lucy about the Santa Claus who visited in May!

XII
GRADUATION

Even before Hazel set foot inside Barrett Elementary School to begin her last year there, she already dreaded her graduation from eighth grade, some nine months off.

Father, still as immovable as Mount Hood, would surely refuse to commit himself again, leaving the girl to endure humdrum afternoons, while her classmates enjoyed themselves at Rockford Grange. At least Ed Callahan would share her plight.

The thought that worried the girl most, however, was of the graduation program itself. She and Ed had weathered many assemblies, sitting inconspicuously together on a back bench, but graduation would be a different story. When her turn came to receive a diploma she would have to march in front of a roomful of wondering faces. Then everyone would realize that she had not participated in the program. Perhaps they would think she was something less than an honor student. Whatever their thoughts, no thirteen-year-old girl would enjoy being singled out as *different.*

Hazel flushed with worry — and anger. "I wish Dad wasn't so stubborn!" she growled to herself.

Each passing day brought the girl closer and closer to the dreaded time.

Meanwhile, life went on. Autumn tiptoed softly over the valley that year, letting Indian Summer linger awhile. It was well into November before the trees shed enough foliage to allow Hazel to see beyond the schoolyard to the nearest house on Methodist Lane. She gazed dreamily at the two-story while sharpening a pencil.

"They must be having a family reunion down there," she surmised from the scene. A number of people, dressed as colorfully as the leaves at their feet, milled around a large picnic table near the house.

All of a sudden, Hazel caught sight of what looked like smoke oozing through an upstairs window.

"Mrs. Yarroll!" she called excitedly. "I think that house is on fire!"

The teacher whirled around and, in seconds, stood at the girl's side. "You're right, Hazel!" The woman's voice remained surprisingly calm as she handed out orders. "Ed, race over to that house at once and warn those poor people! Mary Jo and Arlene, the nearest telephone's at Rockford Store. Hurry up there and call the fire department!"

Before she finished her sentence all three students had vanished through the doorway.

Hazel could see Ed's carrottop head bobbing below as he scurried toward Methodist Lane. The girls, too, were stirring up dust between the schoolhouse and road.

The rest of the students crowded around Hazel and the teacher at the windows.

"Look!" Lucy Trent shouted. "You can see flames now, and those people are partying as if nothing's wrong —"

"They don't realize what's going on above their heads," Mrs. Yarroll explained.

At once a chorus of shouting children filled the air as they tried to warn the family, but to no avail.

Hazel focused on the flames that lashed out angrily at the clear, autumn sky. Goosebumps marched up and down her back while she tried to ignore the sick knawing of fear in the pit of her stomach.

A hush had fallen over her classmates as everyone watched, wide-eyed and alert, from the upper-story.

When Ed reached the scene, picnickers scattered in all directions like a colony of frightened ants. Some climbed in and out of windows, some pulled furniture from doorways, and some fled up the road.

Everything that followed — the fire engine, the spectators — lost importance compared to the terrible flames. The house had turned into a giant torch that burned uncontrollably until everything was consumed. Hazel could see firemen standing around, helpless.

When Ed returned to the classroom, soot covered the freckles on his sober face. "It was too late, Teacher. I — I tried." His voice broke with a sob.

"I know, Ed." Mrs. Yarroll smiled at the boy. "Go wash up!"

He turned away from his staring classmates. They, like Hazel, were stunned. Was this Ed — the class clown?

For the rest of the day, Mrs. Yarroll was unusually lenient about regular studies. And the children were free to wander back and forth to the windows.

As soon as class was dismissed, Hazel and Lucy chose Methodist Lane for their route home that afternoon.

Tall fir trees cast shadows across the charred remains of the house. Smoke still curled up from the embers. Hazel noticed the picnic table, decked with flowers, standing untouched next to the ruins. A lone man sat there, his bewildered face reflecting the awful scene.

A chilling east wind blew upon the Columbia River that winter, causing ice floes that crippled river traffic again. Not everyone frowned at the freezing temperatures, however. The students delighted in the frozen irrigation ditches that bordered the schoolyard. Even without skates, Hazel could glide easily in her rubber boots along the slick ice — a perfect skating rink!

When the valley warmed and waters gushed freely from the mountains again, hundreds of fish filled the irrigation ditches. Because Hazel and

Lucy were considered "big eighth graders," they were allowed to eat their lunches beside the water. Every day they shared a portion of their sandwiches with the fish. As they did, an interesting thing occurred. After several days one particular fish began to return at noontime, waiting expectantly for his lunch of crumbs.

"Isn't that incredible?" Lucy giggled. "And I thought fish were the dumbest creatures on earth."

Hazel didn't seem as interested as her friend. "Lucy, do you know that in a few months we'll be graduating?"

"Yes! Won't that be wonderful?"

"I don't know," Hazel mused. "We won't be returning to Barrett anymore. I'll miss this place."

"But we'll be in high school. Just think of it! We'll be bigwigs then."

Hazel forced a laugh. "I think I'll always feel like a little wig. It'll be scary facing all those other high school kids from all over the valley. There'll be hundreds of them."

Lucy sighed. "You're right. It'll be scary. But Hazel, if you and I still pal around in high school, we'll have each other. Then it won't be so bad."

Hazel's only reply was a faint smile. She didn't admit to her friend what was really troubling her — graduation itself. The dreaded program that she couldn't participate in was getting closer by the day.

A surprise awaited Hazel on her return from school that afternoon. "Grandma Weston!" the girl cried.

"Big Enough!" The woman hugged her granddaughter.

Hazel gazed up at the tall, stately lady. Her hair was a bit grayer, but otherwise, she looked the same as she did years ago in the town of Joseph. The girl would never forget the time Grandma Weston jumped around on a table, screeching fearfully at a harmless mouse.

After the woman explained that she was on her way by train to a meeting in Portland, a round of continuous talking followed.

Finally, Hazel was able to slip a few words into the conversation. After all, she was nearly a grownup now. "Grandma, how are Aunt Maggie and Uncle Emery?"

"They moved back to the Imnaha, you know. Emery's still raising horses. But ever since Maggie had that awful boil on her leg, she hasn't been well. I think it weakened her constitution."

Grandma Smith handed the visitor a cup of tea. "What do you mean?" she asked.

"She just isn't the same strong Maggie we used to know."

Grandma Smith frowned. "How odd! She's never mentioned this in her letters."

"Of course not!" Grandma Weston said. "She wouldn't want to worry you."

Hazel hung her head. She hated to hear bad news about her favorite aunt.

For the next couple of hours the house bubbled with friendly, hurried chatter. The visitor would have to return to the train station shortly, and all too soon Hazel was sandwiched between her grandmothers, riding toward town.

Mother turned to Grandma Weston. "It's a shame your meeting wasn't a bit later in the year. Then you could have seen Hazel graduate from eighth grade."

"Eighth grade!" gasped the elderly woman. "Are you that old already. Child?"

"Yes, Ma'am." Hazel stiffened as she thought, "I'm glad she won't be here to see me make a spectacle of myself."

One warm May afternoon, Hazel was greeted by more visitors in her living room — Mrs. Hodson and Edith.

"Hazel!" Edith exclaimed. "I've been accepted for nursing school in the fall!"

Hazel beamed back at her friend. "Congratulations, Edith!"

"I'm so excited, I can't wait," the older girl said.

"Well, I can!" laughed her mother. "I'll be over my head in sewing to get you ready for school." Then the pretty lady looked directly at Hazel. "I was just beginning to tell your mother the awful experience I had this afternoon."

Hazel sat down and listened to Mrs. Hodson, appreciating the fact that the woman always included the girl in the conversation.

Mrs. Hodson began her story, "I had been scrubbing the kitchen floor half the day. It was a mess. Well, I had this filthy wash water in a bucket and threw it out the door, as always. But this time, Mr. Backer happened to round the corner at that exact moment — and he was wearing his Sunday suit! The poor man caught that dirty water full in the face!"

"Oh, no!" Hazel groaned.

"Why was he dressed up on a Friday afternoon, Lena?" Mother asked.

"It seems he was on his way to a funeral and needed my husband because they were short one pallbearer. Oh, I was so embarrassed!"

Hazel piped up, "Was Mr. Backer angry, Mrs. Hodson?"

"He certainly had a right to be with that nasty water dripping down his best suit. But that man is one, true Christian. He just turned around and went back home to change clothes. When he returned for Joe, I was still too embarrassed to face him."

"Don't be so hard on yourself, Lena!" Mother consoled the neighbor. "Accidents do happen, you know." Then she quickly changed the subject.

Soon the neighbors excused themselves to leave. "Do drop over and visit me more often, Ida!" Mrs. Hodson said. "I miss your company since Kelly's been born."

"I'll try, Lena. Thank you!" Mother replied.

Hazel grinned at Edith as the older girl's springy steps revealed her glad heart.

Every member of the Hodson family seemed to radiate a special quality that Hazel couldn't quite identify. The girl recalled the time that young Harv Hodson and his mother answered her questions with the Bible. She longed for the same kind of knowledge they possessed. Ever since that time, there was a stirring within Hazel, a stirring that would return again and again as she grew closer to the Hodson family.

When the inevitable graduation practice began, Hazel and Ed were again given extra study time in the deserted schoolroom.

151

On one such afternoon, Mrs. Yarroll called Hazel up to her desk. "I have good news for you. Yesterday, the State examiner informed me that you'll be able to skip your State final in geography because of your high grades in that subject throughout the years.

Hazel was speechless, but grinned proudly.

"Now that should give you more time to study your spelling," Mrs. Yarroll continued.

Hazel's radiant expression suddenly turned sour.

The teacher noticed. "I think if you could get a *B* on your spelling final, you'd have one of the highest grade averages in our graduation class. It's a shame you can't participate in the program."

"Yes, Ma'am!" Hazel murmured. "But I'm glad Dad's so honest. He can't promise he'll be at the program. After all, an emergency or something might come up." Hazel shuffled her feet awkwardly at the teacher's desk.

Her words sounded nice, but inside, frustration tied Hazel into knots.

The following week final exams were given, then sent off to the State examiner. That same week Kelly celebrated his third birthday.

Although Hazel received excellent grades in her final exams — except spelling — nothing seemed to cheer her, not even the new dress Mother had made for graduation. The girl's every waking hour became obsessed with worry about what should have been a happy occasion. She dreaded diploma time. She would rather be locked in a hot kitchen with fourteen bushels of peaches to can than to parade in front of all those strangers and have them wonder why she and Ed were left out of the main program.

When the fateful night arrived, Hazel's stomach felt like a runaway butter churn. She plopped down next to Ed on "their bench" behind the other graduates and gazed out at the spectators flooding the hall. Hazel scrunched down trying to make herself small and unassuming. She felt somewhat better after she spotted Lucy Trent smiling at her from a blur of pastels.

As the sun dipped behind the mountains, every mosquito in the valley must have decided to attend Barrett eighth-grade graduation, because they turned out in swarms.

Hazel and Ed took turns swatting at the pesky creatures, pretending to pay little attention to the program in front of them.

At last Mrs. Yarroll began handing out diplomas in alphabetical order.

"Ed Callahan!" came the teacher's voice.

The grinning boy strolled up to the lectern in his usual, lackadaisical way.

153

Hazel wished she could be that carefree, while she tried to still her pounding heart.

On and on the teacher's voice droned as she called the names of each graduate. Then finally — "Hazel Weston!"

The girl rose slowly from her seat and started toward the teacher. Her knees felt rubbery and her feet lagged. Mrs. Yarroll seemed to be standing at the end of a long, long corridor. The further the girl walked, the longer the corridor stretched out ahead of her. Staring eyes pressed in from every direction, squeezing the very breath from her lungs. Hazel's nightmare had come true, but it was worse than a nightmare. It was real, and she could almost hear the whole audience thinking, "Is this girl such a poor student that she can't participate in the program? What awful deed has she done to deserve such exclusion?"

Finally, Hazel felt the teacher's hand clasp hers. Then Mrs. Yarroll's voice floated out into the room like music, "I want you parents and relatives to realize that Miss Weston here is one of my best students. In fact, her geography grades were so good that the State examiner allowed her to be exempt from the final in that subject. Now, that is an accomplishment!"

The room exploded into a jubilant clapping sound, and in that moment all the girl's turmoil of the past months melted away. Hugging her diploma, Hazel walked back to her seat, basking in the sound of a thunderous applause.

Even though she couldn't participate in the program, she now felt a part of it — the best part!

Riding home in the car afterward, Hazel found it hard to concentrate on Mother and Grandma's quiet conversation. The girl was lost in a world of her own.

A full moon had risen over the eastern ridge, making Mount Hood brilliant, like a cluster of diamonds. Very few stars blinked through the night sky.

Five years' worth of memories sailed to her on a soft, summer breeze — the valley buried beneath deep snowdrifts, the valley bursting into full bloom, the valley ripe with succulent fruit. The girl thought of Holly and Margie and sledrides by moonlight.

The land almost seemed human to her, sometimes warm and cordial, sometimes ill-tempered. Hazel had grown to love the place, not as a "dream valley" anymore, but for its true self — in spite of its faults. After all, real friends were to love that way.

Then Grandma's voice rang out, "Come on, Girl — we're home!"

THE END

ABOUT THE AUTHOR

Paula Montgomery lives with her logger-husband, their two children, and any other youngsters who happen to occupy their mountain-top home in Washington state.

Midway between the snowcapped peaks of Mount Hood and Mount Adams, the Montgomerys enjoy a splendid view of the Columbia River Gorge and its surrounding fertile lands — great inspiration for an author.

Mrs. Montgomery became serious about writing at Frederick Community College in Maryland. There she edited literary magazines while working on her Associate of Arts Degree. She graduated in 1965.

Although she has written for such publications as *These Times* and *Insight,* children's literature remains her favorite. Mrs. Montgomery has contributed many stories to *Guide,* an inspirational magazine for juniors, and she hopes to produce more non-fiction books for that age group as often as "time and mothering" permit.